Introducing... Sasha Abramowitz

Introducing... Sasha Abramowitz

SUE HALPERN

Frances Foster Books

Farrar Straus Giroux New York

Copyright © 2005 by Sue Halpern
All rights reserved
Distributed in Canada by Douglas & McIntyre Publishing Group
Printed in the United States of America
Designed by Nancy Goldenberg
First edition, 2005
1   3   5   7   9   10   8   6   4   2

www.fsgkidsbooks.com

Library of Congress Cataloging-in-Publication Data
Halpern, Sue.
    Introducing . . . Sasha Abramowitz / Sue Halpern.— 1st ed.
        p.   cm.
    Summary: Memoir of the 12th year of Sasha's life, when she comes to accept
that her older brother's problems make her different, but no different from
anyone else.
    ISBN-13: 978-0-374-38432-6
    ISBN-10: 0-374-38432-0
    [1. Tourette syndrome—Fiction.   2. Friendship—Fiction.
3. Interpersonal relations—Fiction.]   I. Title.

PZ7.H16673In 2005
[Fic]—dc22

                                                         2004053269

For Sophie Crane McKibben

Introducing...
Sasha
Abramowitz

Call me . . . Sasha. Sasha Abramowitz. That's my name, pretty much. Officially it's Sasha Marie Curie Abramowitz, but I think it's weird having someone else's name sitting right in the middle of my own, even if it is the name of the first woman to win a Nobel Prize, the only one to win it twice. (And get this, Marie Curie was married to a man who also won a Nobel Prize, and they had a daughter who won a Nobel Prize, and that daughter married a man who won a Nobel Prize. So don't you just wonder how her other kid, the only member of the family not to win a Nobel Prize, felt? I'll bet nobody has *her* name parked in the middle of theirs.)

My parents thought it would be inspirational, adding Marie Curie's name to mine, as if somehow her greatness would rub off on me. When I used to complain, my father would shake his head regretfully and say, "You know, Sasha, we came very close to giving you her maiden name, too, but there just wasn't room enough on the birth certificate." I guess you have to be thankful for the little things. Like not being named Sasha Marie Sklodowska Curie Abramowitz.

Though it's probably too early to say for sure, I don't think their plan is working, because even though I'm only eleven, I kind of doubt I'm going to grow up to be a chemist (Marie Curie's Nobel Prize #1) or a physicist (Nobel Prize #2). I want to be a writer. A writer and, maybe, a pastry chef. Personally, I think they should have given a Nobel Prize to the person who discovered double fudge brownies. The kind without nuts. Putting nuts in brownies was a *very bad idea* and, not to be too mean, I truly hope the person who came up with it lived to regret it.

My mother, believe it or not, loves nuts—walnuts, in particular. She says that viewed sideways they sort of look like the hippocampus, which she also loves. When I was really little I thought the hippocampus was some sort of large African mammal (how it also looked like a walnut, I couldn't tell you). It turns out, though, to be part of the brain, which is what she studies—the parts of the brain that have to do with memory. (You should see her lab. It's gross.) Mom and Dad are both teachers at Krieger College, which is where we live, in a dorm. They're the dorm parents, which means that when dopey Caroline Fleck locks herself out of her room again, or when sad sack Tommy Mendoza is dumped by his girlfriend (also again, though I don't think I'm supposed to know that), or it looks like Jillian Kramer, who has perfect hair and perfect skin and perfect clothes, is not going to pass Spanish, my parents try to help them out. They unlock Caroline's door, and give Tommy a hug and a glass of chocolate milk, and get Jillian a tutor. Kids bang on our door day and night, but especially night, which always makes our dog, Tripod, howl, with one exception: when she smells Frank Benjamin coming. Tripod always knows it's him and lies down, rolls over, and madly waves her three legs in the air before even one of Frank's knuckles has touched wood. (Fact: No one ever says what happened to the other leg. By the time I came along, it just wasn't there.) Frank says that for his senior project he is going to make a fourth leg for Tripod that will work and look just like a regular leg, but actually will be a small computer. The only problem with this, I keep telling him, is that then Tripod can't be called Tripod, because she will no longer be a three-legged dog.

"No need to be so literal, Sasha," my father says. "The world has room for a four-legged Tripod."

That is typical of my father, who is a poet. He writes poetry for two hours every day at the barbershop downtown. They even have a special chair reserved for him. He says it's the best place to write because it has "atmosphere." He says his office at the college, where he teaches English, is too dull. "It's not a good medium for fermenting the creative juices," he tells people, which makes it sound like he's making cider, not poems.

My father likes words. He likes how sometimes there is only one word in the whole world that will say the thing that needs to be said—and how sometimes words are runny like watercolors. Since I was little we've played the "Like" game, which is not about what I like (double fudge brownies, obviously) but about making word pictures. We started with clouds: "That cloud looks like . . . a dolphin. That cloud looks like . . . a peach. That cloud looks like . . . Mount Shasta." Then we moved to trees and bushes: "That tree looks like hands reaching out to God. That tree looks like an arrow. That bush looks like an old woman wearing a housecoat." Everything is fair game: "Those olives are staring at me like a pair of vacant eyes," Dad said to me one night when we were putting out vegetables and dip for a college party. "The wind is howling on the other side of the door like an impatient wolf," I told him during a really bad storm.

It's a good game. We play it a lot in the car, especially when we're driving to Massachusetts to visit my brother. That's another thing about me: I have a brother. His name is Daniel. He's six years older than I am and goes to a special school for kids who are sick. Not sick in the throwing-up kind of way, but sick as in their minds don't work quite right. So that's the last thing you should know about me, at least for now: I have a brother and he has "problems."

2

Don't feel sorry for me or think I'm a freak just because my brother is who he is. And don't feel sorry for him or
think he's a freak, either. That's what my parents say: "Don't
feel sorry for him, Sasha; what is, is," even though I do feel
sorry for him. I feel sorry for him every single day of the year,
and especially on his birthday, when I wonder if he feels sorry
that he was even born. "He doesn't think that way," my
mother says, but how does she know? Even if she studies the
brain, does that make her a mind reader?

Here's the thing about Danny: he didn't always go to
Trannell Academy, and we didn't always live in the dorm at
Krieger College. Danny used to live with us, in our house,
which was a real house, a three-bedroom split-level with a
pretty big backyard and one of those aboveground swimming
pools with a redwood deck around it. The people we bought

the house from put it in and they would have taken it away with them, too, if they weren't moving to Idaho or Montana, I don't remember which, but someplace cold. And if they had taken the pool, we might still be living there and Danny wouldn't be at Trannell, though you can never know these things for sure. Still, I think it was the pool that did it, the pool that got things going in the direction they went. "The swimming pool is like a snowball," I said once to my father, but he said, "No, I don't see it. You haven't painted a clear enough picture." But how clear did he need it to be? A snowball rolls down a hill, picking up more and more snow, getting bigger and bigger, mowing down everything in its path. He, of all people, should have known that.

We moved to that house when I was two and Danny was eight, so I don't really remember living anywhere else, even though we came from New York City, which you would think might have impressed itself on my brain. All those taxis honking their horns, all those car alarms, all those streetlights, all those restaurant smells. My mother didn't want to make the move. She had grown up there and didn't see why we shouldn't, too. It was where she had gone to grade school and high school and college and graduate school. She had a good job there, at Columbia University, which is where she met my father, who had grown up in New Jersey.

"Leaves," my father would say, making his case for moving out of the city. (At least, this is what he told me.) "Grass. Fresh air."

"Hay fever," my mother would reply. "Ragweed. Pollen. Mucus." (Actually, I'm not sure she said "mucus," but she probably thought it. That, and "tissues." She is very germ-conscious.)

Even though we eventually left the city, it wasn't because my father had won the argument or my mother had lost. It was because of Danny, when they found out.

My mother says that maybe if she hadn't been a brain re-searcher, she would have figured out about Danny sooner. "The brain is so *various*," she likes to say, meaning that be-cause everyone's brain is different, people are different—they behave differently, they are interested in different things, they learn things at different paces. (No kidding: I'm really good at math, but my handwriting stinks and I can't seem to make it any better no matter how hard I try.) My father gets mad when my mother says she should have known sooner, because, he says, she is blaming herself. "It is a pointless exercise," he tells her, which doesn't make her cry any less. (Fact: One good thing about my parents: they don't usually pretend every-thing is okay when it isn't.)

I think maybe they were sidetracked about Danny because he was so cute. I mean, really. Danny was one of the cutest ba-bies in the history of the world. I've seen the pictures. He had big green eyes and shiny red cheeks and curly black hair. And he was easy. Mom says he was a much easier baby than I was. (Apparently, I had a lot of gas.) He wasn't especially demand-ing. He actually seemed to like lying on his back in his crib for hours at a time and would get mad if someone tried to move him. Mom says it was like he was thinking, like he was solving one of the great mysteries of the universe or some particularly difficult equation.

"What did I know?" she told me. "I never had children before. I didn't have brothers or sisters. It was all new to me, and of course all parents assume their baby is a genius, the next Einstein."

"You mean the next Marcia Abramowitz," I said, referring to my mom. She is really smart. She's so smart it scares me sometimes.

My mom blushed. She has the same pale skin and curly black hair as Danny. I favor my dad, which is to say I'm not as good-looking as those two. My hair is the color of tree bark, and my eyes are basically black. My parents tell me I'm beautiful, of course, but one night I heard Dad tell Mom that I was going to grow up to be one of those girls people say look "interesting," which I didn't exactly take as a compliment.

"So how did you figure it out?" I asked my mom. "About Danny, I mean."

You know how in every family there are some stories that get told over and over again—like the time Aunt Ida got locked in the bathroom on the Amtrak train and had to climb out the window at Union Station, or the one about the trip to Disneyland, when Mickey Mouse accidentally stepped on Billy's toe? Well, in our family those stories are almost always about Danny, and my favorite (not favorite because I like it the best, but favorite because I want to hear it the most) is the one where my parents finally understood what was what.

This is how Daddy tells it: He'd taken my brother to a Mets game. Danny was seven. The Mets were losing, and everyone in the bleachers was yelling and screaming. During the seventh-inning stretch, right after they sang "Take Me Out to the Ball Game," a man on the other side of Danny leaned over to my dad and said, "Pretty unusual kid you've got there." Daddy was just about to thank him, because in our family "unusual" is a synonym for "great," but before he could, the man said, "I didn't know how to cuss like that till I was in the Navy." Daddy had had his headphones on for most of the game, so he hadn't heard Danny himself. (Believe it or not, Daddy listens to the game on the radio even when he's in the stadium watching it so he can hear what the commentators are saying.) But when the game started up again he kept them off, and sure enough, every once in a while Danny let loose a string of words that according to Daddy would make a grown man blush. Later, when Daddy told my mother about it, she said, "Were the Mets winning or losing?" "What kind of a question is that?" Daddy said, pretty annoyed, and then he added, "Losing. But it was very close." And then Mom said, "Coprolalia," and Dad made a joke, saying, "No, Bobby Bonilla was in right field." Then Mom got mad and said, "Get serious, Barney. Coprolalia means repetitive swearing. It can be triggered by stress. It's usually a sign of a

11

serious neurological problem." And the rest is history. (Translation: The rest is everything that happened after that. The doctors they saw, the tests they did, the schools Danny was in, the kids who wouldn't play with him, the medicines he had to take. Et cetera, et cetera, et cetera.)

My doctor, who I call the Eraser, even though the sign outside his office reads EDGAR RAYMOND SERKOWSKY, M.D., says the reason I want to hear this story is because I want to make sure that I am not going to turn out like Danny. He has a point, which for me is saying a lot, since I'm not exactly a big fan of the Eraser's. He always wants to talk about my feelings, as if by talking about them they'll go away or something. (Note: That's why I call E. RAYmond SERkowsky the Eraser.) How does it feel to have a brother like Danny, he wants to know. How does it feel to have a brother who has to go to a place like Trannell? How does it feel to visit him there? I know it's not really the Eraser's fault—asking questions like that is just his job—but the truth is, most of the time I'd rather not talk about it. It's bad enough having a brother who isn't normal, but then to be forced to discuss it out loud, with a stranger? Not that he's a stranger anymore. It's been three years, and mostly when I go there we talk about the Eraser's cats, Tom and Jerry, and how he grew up in a lumber camp somewhere in Canada where his father was the foreman, and what books I happen to be reading at the time or what movies I've seen or what's going on at school. I think he thinks I don't notice it when he sneaks in questions about me and my family, but how could I not? The fact is, I've got a kind of radar for questions like that.

I used to be embarrassed to have to see the Eraser twice a month: If someone I knew saw me going into his office, what would they think? I wanted to wear a sign that said I'M NOT COMING HERE TO TALK ABOUT ME. I'M ALL RIGHT. When I mentioned this to the Eraser he said, "So, Sasha, do you resent Danny?" which made me want to scream at him, *"Of course I resent Danny. Wouldn't you?"* But instead I just looked at him sideways and said, innocently, "Why?"

The Eraser is not stupid. I mean, he knew I was lying.

3

Have you ever noticed how everyone is always telling you to be honest all the time, and then how everyone lies? Either they say things that are just untrue, or they don't contradict someone else who says something that's untrue. (Note: "Contradict" was one of my vocabulary words this year, and my teacher, Mrs. Blank—I'm not lying, her name really is Mrs. Blank—encourages us to use our vocabulary words in our writing.) I'm not saying that I don't do this, too. I mean, look at me and the Eraser. He says, "Do you resent your brother?" and I say no, and pretend I don't have any idea what he's talking about. That's Lie #1. He knows I'm lying and doesn't say anything about it. That's Lie #2. Instead, he changes the subject and says, "Tom got his tail caught in the closet door and had to go to the vet. The vet said we should let him sleep with us that night so we could monitor his pain. Boy, did that make Jerry mad."

"What did Jerry do?" I asked, thinking less about the cat than about the Eraser and his wife lying in bed, and wondering if he sleeps in his underwear like my dad.

"He didn't do anything," the Eraser said.

"He didn't do anything?" I repeated. "If he didn't do anything, how do you know he was mad?"

"It was obvious," he said. "In the morning Jerry wanted nothing to do with Tom. He just pretended Tom wasn't there. Even when Tom sat on Jerry's head, Jerry pretended he wasn't there. Or that he was a hat. I don't know."

Fact: The Eraser is always admitting what he doesn't know. But that's basically a lie, too. "I don't know how you're feeling, Sasha," he says all the time. "I need you to tell me."

But why does he need me to tell him? What does he care?

"He cares because it is his job to care," my father says. "Plus, how could he not care about you? You're Sasha Abramowitz." He says this as if I were Eleanor Roosevelt[1] or Queen Elizabeth—someone famous like that.

---

1. I used to wish that if my parents had to put somebody else's name in the middle of mine, it would be Eleanor Roosevelt's. They said there were already girls with E.R.'s name in theirs, and that Marie Curie was more "distinctive." "Distinctive" was the thing I didn't like, but never mind. When I did my report on Eleanor Roosevelt (see Appendix 1), though, I found that she and Madame Curie were related in a way. They both died from the same disease: aplastic anemia (see Appendix 2).

(This, by the way, is a footnote. In our writing class we are learning how to do footnotes and other things for research papers, and Mrs. Blank says that we should practice using them "at every opportunity." So here it is, my opportunity.)

"Not famous, Sasha," Daddy says. "Special. You're special."

"All parents think their kid is special," my best friend, Carla, says when I repeat this conversation to her. Carla is a good person to talk to about things like this—she has *four* parents. There's her mom, Judy, and her stepfather, Janusz (I know, it's a weird name), and then there's her dad, Cliff, and her stepmother, Janice (which makes it even weirder, since "Janusz" is pronounced kind of like "Janice"). Carla says it's as if her parents got divorced and then remarried the same person. (But that's just a joke. Janusz is old and from Poland. Janice is not old, and I don't know where she's from—possibly Connecticut, or Kansas. She's nice, though.) If you think the name thing is a little strange, try this: they all live together in a duplex about a block from the college campus. They're all teachers at Krieger College, too.

"Duplex" is not one of this year's vocabulary words, not yet, anyway, and I had never heard it till Judy and Cliff got divorced and sold their house on College Circle and bought the one on Krieger Avenue. It used to be the old college infirmary, and when I say "old," I mean *old*. When Carla's father was fixing up the kitchen on the ground floor (Janusz and Judy fixed up the one on the second floor), he found newspapers from 1914 stuffed in the walls for insulation.

So Cliff and Janice have the first floor, Judy and Janusz have the second floor, and Carla has this really cool room they made for her in the attic. She's got a telescope, which Janusz, who is an astronomer, actually built, and a hammock that Cliff brought back from Brazil (he studies tropical plants and animals), and a trundle bed, which is where I sleep when I spend the night. Half the week Carla has breakfast and dinner with her mom and stepfather, and half the week she has breakfast and dinner with her dad and stepmother. Half the week her dad packs her lunch and does all the carpooling, and then they switch, and her mother packs her lunch and does all the carpooling. Carla calls it "the changing of the guard." She says it's all right, having so many adults in the house, because then she almost never has to have a babysitter.

Still, she has to admit, my babysitter, Andrew, is the best, the very best, and the weird thing is that it was Carla, really, who introduced us. Not introduced in the usual "Hi, my name is Sasha, what's yours?" kind of way, but in a totally unusual, pretty much unlikely way. It started with *Harriet the Spy*. Carla read it and loved it. I read it, too, but I didn't love it as much, I guess, as Carla did, because when she was finished, she went back to the beginning and started reading it all over. Okay, I know what you're thinking: You're thinking, "So what, I did that with *Harry Potter*. I did that with *Mr. Popper's Penguins*. I did that with *Ramona*. What's the big deal? The big deal is that when Carla finished *Harriet the Spy* the second time, she was sure—sure of what she was going to be, and not just when she grew up, but right then and there. Carla was going to be a private eye. " 'Private eye' is another way of saying 'spy,' " Carla explained, "but it sounds more like a job."

"Carla Smith, private eye," I said, trying it out. "Not bad."

"Not bad?" Carla said loudly. "Ewww. It's awful." We were in the middle of art class, working on posters for Earth Day.

"Carla Smith," Mrs. Blank said, walking hastily in our direction. Our desks are in the center of room 6B, so everyone was watching. "I want you to apologize to Sasha this instant, and tell her how much you *admire* her poster." Mrs. Blank is really into "put-ups," not "put-downs," and for emphasis she made the word "admire," which when I last checked had two syllables, "ad" and "mire," into a three- or four-syllable word. Something like "ad-mmm-iiii-rrrrrrr." Carla looked at me and smiled sweetly. "Sorry, Sasha," she said.

"Sorry, Sasha *what?*" Mrs. Blank said.

"Sorry, Sasha, your poster is really nice," Carla said, rolling her eyes when Mrs. Blank had turned around and was on her way back to her desk. I rolled my eyes, too. The truth is, I'm a lousy artist. It has something to do with my lousy handwriting, which has to do with having lousy fine motor skills. At least, that's what I heard Mom say to Dad, to explain why until three years ago, when I was eight, I still had to have help tying my shoes. She also said it didn't matter, I'd probably outgrow it.

"I don't get it," I said to Carla when we had put our art supplies away and were sitting outside at the edge of the playground, eating lunch. "What's wrong with 'Carla Smith, private eye'? I thought you wanted to be a private eye."

"Oh no!" Carla said, scrunching up her face. "Janusz made my sandwich."

For a moment I didn't know if she meant Janusz or Janice, but when she peeled back the bread and showed me the liverwurst, I knew it was him, not her.

"You want it?" she asked, pushing the sandwich in my direction.

"No, thanks," I said. "I don't eat liver."

"I don't think it's real liver," Carla said, pushing it a little closer.

"Get it away from me," I said, pushing it back. For some reason this reminded me of Danny and me, when we were little. Or, rather, when I was little, since he's never seemed little to me. When *I* was little, Danny liked to mix up disgusting concoctions of things like dead mosquitoes and worms in mud and serve them to me, insisting that they were real food.

"I do want to be a private eye," Carla said, picking up the conversation that I wasn't sure we'd ever get through. "I *am* a private eye," she said, reaching into her backpack and taking out a manila envelope. She opened the clasp, pulled out a small card, and handed it to me. It said: DREW HARDY AND ASSOCIATES, PRIVATE INVESTIGATORS. NO JOB TOO SMALL. NO JOB TOO BIG. SERVING THE KRIEGER COMMUNITY SINCE 1992, and had a phone number at the bottom. *My* phone number.

"What about *your* phone number?" I protested.

"You know how hard it is for me to get messages," Carla protested back. "You only have to live with two absent-minded professors. I have to live with four! Anyhow, you're the associate."

"Thanks for letting me know," I said, pretending to be angry, but secretly I was pleased. If Carla was going to be a spy, I wanted to be one, too.

"What's this about serving the Krieger community since 1992? We were born in 1992."

"My point exactly," said Carla, just as the bell rang and we had to rush back into school and change for gym. Why we have gym right after lunch, I'll never know.

" 'Carla Smith' is not a good name for a private eye," Carla explained while we were lacing up our sneakers. "It's too dull. I mean, would you hire someone named Carla Smith? I wouldn't. Anyway, I figure 'Drew Hardy' has better name recognition."

"Name recognition?" I asked.

"Yeah," she said. "Like when you go to the bookstore. Do you look for a book by someone you've never heard of, or do you see if an author you like has another book out?"

"Carla and Sasha, are you planning on joining us?" Mrs. Blank called. The whole rest of the class was lined up by the door, ready to go outside and play kickball. We were holding them up.

"Sorry," we said in unison.

"If people don't look for books by someone they've never heard of," I whispered to Carla as we walked out to the playing field, "how will new authors ever get known?" This was a particularly sore subject for me, since I want to be a writer, and what if I never had "name recognition" and nobody ever read my stories?

"That's not the point," Carla whispered back.

"What is the point?" I asked when we were walking home from school.

"The point," said Carla, stopping in the middle of the sidewalk and grabbing hold of my shoulders, "is that everyone has heard of Nancy Drew and the Hardy Boys. Name me one person that has never heard of them."

It occurred to me that maybe Danny didn't know about them. As smart as he is, and he is very, very smart, he's never been much of a reader. I didn't say this, though. In matters like this, Danny didn't count.

"But they're just characters in a book!" I said. (Note to the Eraser: Do you know the word "exasperated"? That's how I *felt*. Exasperated.)

"First of all," Carla said, "they were very successful characters. They always solved their cases, and they had a lot of them. Second," she said, taking her hands off my shoulders, "I can't believe you said that. You. They're *just* characters? I thought you wanted to be a writer."

About five days after Carla showed me "our" business cards, my mother knocked on my bedroom door and handed me the phone. She had a funny look on her face.

"I think it's one of my students," she said with her hand over the receiver.

I mouthed the word "Why?"

She shrugged and handed me the phone. College kids do all sorts of strange stuff, like wear their sunglasses on the back of their head and walk around in shorts during a snowstorm. When you live with them, like we do, you learn to ignore it.

"Is this Drew Hardy?" a male voice said.

For a minute I didn't know what he was talking about, and was just going to tell him he had the wrong number when I remembered. "Sort of," I said. "I mean, you've got the right number."

"I've got a mystery for you to solve," he said. I sat up straight. A mystery? Already? Carla was not going to believe it.

"Okay," I said, realizing that being the associate was no small thing. I mean, here I was, talking to our first client.

"The mystery is," he went on, "why is someone on the Krieger campus going around saying I'm a private investigator?"

"Someone is saying *you're* a private investigator? I don't get it," I said.

"It was posted on the bulletin board in Daisy South," he said. (Daisy South, by the way, is one of the Krieger dorms. At Krieger, all the dorms are named for flowers. It was Erasmus Krieger's idea, to remind people that "here at Krieger, minds are always in bloom." We live in Aster West, which I think is better than living in Poppy, or Petunia, or Chrysanthemum, which are the dorms nearest ours.)

"*What* was posted?" I asked, even though I knew. I was the one who had put our business cards in every laundry room on campus.

"Drew Hardy and Associates, Private Investigators," he said, reading the card, and then paused. I paused, too. What was he getting at?

"I'm Drew Hardy," he said. "Andrew Hardy. Krieger College senior class."

"Oh," I said. I was stalling for time, trying to think fast.

"The problem is," he went on, "that I just had business

cards printed up myself, and I was planning to leave them all over campus and in town this weekend."

"Are you a private eye, too?" I asked. How much of a coincidence was that? ("Coincidence"—another vocabulary word.)

Andrew laughed. "No, I'm a magician. I do card tricks. I was hoping to earn some extra money doing birthday parties for faculty brats, that sort of thing."

"O-kay," I said, taking a sharp breath. I hate it when those of us who happen to have parents who happen to be on the faculty are called *brats*.

"Not okay," he said. "People are going to get confused when they see cards for Drew Hardy, private eye, and Andrew Hardy, magician. It's going to be bad for business. They're going to think I'm coming into their homes to snoop on them. It's not going to work, and I really need the money. I was counting on it."

Andrew didn't sound mad so much as desperate. He sounded like Tripod when she whines, very quietly, under the table on Thanksgiving. There hasn't been a Thanksgiving when we haven't given her a bowl of turkey, gravy, mashed potatoes, and stuffing, and yet Tripod always whines, every year.

"Look, if you need to make some money right away, I know how you can," I said.

"How?"

"Hang up and call this number back in exactly three minutes and ask for Professor Abramowitz."

24

"Which Professor Abramowitz, Mr. or Mrs.?"

"Either one will do. They're my parents and they have tickets for a dance performance tonight, and Mom thought Dad had lined up a babysitter, and Dad thought Mom had, and Ellie Anderson, my usual babysitter, is sick, so they're basically stuck."

"I don't know. I've never done that before," Andrew said. "What's your name?"

"Sasha," I said. "They pay eight dollars an hour. Plus, if I like you and you like me, they'll call you all the time."

"What about Ellie Anderson?"

"She told Mom she had a lot on her plate this semester, and since she is an incredibly picky eater, I figured she wasn't talking about food."

"You sound okay," Andrew said. I could tell he was warming up to the idea.

"So do you," I said. "We're in Aster West, ground floor. Bring your cards."

5

Andrew turned out to be short, with straight
dark hair and some bristles on his chin that looked more like
he'd forgotten to shave than that he had actually grown a
beard. He was wearing a pair of overalls and a plaid flannel
shirt and a blue-and-gold cap that said KRIEGER BASEBALL.
The Krieger baseball team is pretty famous. Or shall I say
infamous. (Yes, you're right, another vocabulary word.) The
Krieger Cats haven't won a game in seven years. Most people wear Krieger baseball caps as a joke, but not Andrew. He's
on the team. My father recognized him when he opened
the door.

"I know you," Dad said. "You're the shortstop." This was
before Andrew had even stepped into our apartment. But you
have to understand that Dad *loves* baseball. Even Krieger baseball. Maybe, especially, Krieger baseball. You should hear him

go on about how baseball is a great drama, how it's always tragic, how great poetry is made of great tragedy. (Actually, on second thought, maybe you shouldn't.) Dad believes that loving baseball is one of the requirements of being a poet. I can see him pacing back and forth in front of his classroom, telling his students that if they want to be real poets like him they will need a pencil, a pad of paper, a dictionary, and a love of baseball. Knowing Dad, he'd probably say "and a passion for the game," and figure that the true poets in the class would know which game he was referring to.

"And I know *you*," Andrew said, stooping down to pet Tripod.

Everyone at Krieger College knows our dog. A couple of years ago, when she graduated from dog obedience school, the *Krieger Courier* featured her as its "Student of the Week." Dog school taught Tripod good manners ("sit" and "shake hands"), but it didn't cure her of wandering. She is very predictable, though, so it's not even exactly wandering. It's more like migrating. As soon as we let her out, she walks over to the college dining hall and stands by the door on her three feet, looking very sad and very hungry, and pretty soon kids are stopping by with bagels and hot dogs and ice cream and stuff from the salad bar. (Black olives and chickpeas are her favorites.)

"So who is Drew Hardy and when do I get to meet him?" Andrew wanted to know as soon as my parents left.

"Do a card trick first, and then I'll tell you," I said.

"Can I trust you?"

"Of course. I'll even pinkie swear if you want me to."

"No need," Andrew said. "I was just checking."

We were sitting at the kitchen table, waiting for a frozen pizza to heat up. You know the kind—too much crust, lots of cheese that bubbles and burns unless you take it out of the oven at exactly the right moment, which, as far as I can tell, is never.

The kitchen in our apartment is small, but it has windows that open to the garden, where we eat when it gets warmer out. There's also a dining room with a boarded-up dumbwaiter that used to go down to the basement, which is where the kitchen used to be, back in the days when there were servants who cooked all the meals. The apartment itself is really nice. The living room is huge and has wood floors covered with thick old rugs, and wood walls that are lined with the books my parents like the most and probably read the least, since the ones they really need are in their offices. In addition to the living room there is something called "the parlor," which has big overstuffed chairs in it, and a leather couch with a portrait of Erasmus Krieger, the founder of Krieger College, hanging over it. I don't like Erasmus Krieger—meaning I don't like the way he looks. He's got narrow beady eyes, a long face, and a mean expression. It's a rule at the college that every building has to have a picture of the founder in it, which is why that creepy painting is hanging in our place. Of course, if it weren't for Erasmus Krieger there would be no Krieger College and my parents wouldn't have jobs here and we wouldn't live in Aster West and I wouldn't know Carla, or Andrew, for that matter, so I guess I should be grateful. (Thank you, Erasmus.)

I really like my bedroom, though. It's got high ceilings, and Dad built me a loft bed with a swing underneath it. He also built a set of bookcases and a window seat that's also a toy box. Daddy is a really good carpenter. If, for some reason, he couldn't be a poet, I think he'd be one of those guys who wear heavy-duty jeans and have a tool belt hanging off their waist, which is funny, if you know what my dad looks like. He's a little chubby, and bald, and has this thing for bow ties. If you wear bow ties, you probably also wear a button-down shirt and a sport coat, wool in the winter, linen in the summer. That's Dad. People say he is "dapper."

Mom, on the other hand, is sort of frumpy. She doesn't really care what she looks like. Sometimes she doesn't notice what she's put on, like the time she taught a three-hour class wearing nothing but her lab coat, a turtleneck, and her slip because she forgot to put on her jumper. Another time, Mom almost went to a dinner party at the college president's house wearing her dress turned around so that the back was in front and the front was in back.

"I think the buttons look nicer in the front," she told Dad when he pointed out her mistake. "But I was wondering why the belt buckle was in the back. It did seem inconvenient."

(Fact: If you need fashion advice, do not ask my mother.)

The card trick Andrew was going to show me was called Back Flip.[2] He shuffled the cards, arching their backs, then easing them flat again.

"Here," he said, fanning them out. "Pick one."

I pulled one from the far right corner, thinking that maybe this would trip him up. In my experience, people usually pick from the middle. Maybe he was counting on that.

It was the seven of spades. Spades are my favorite suit, after clubs. Clubs are best, I think. They remind me of looking for four-leaf clovers (of which I've found exactly none so far—which may tell you something about the kind of luck I have).

"Okay," Andrew said, holding out the whole deck. "Without telling me which card it is, put it back."

I slid it in. "Good," he said. "Fine." He was looking me right in the eyes. He wasn't smiling at all. It was a little creepy.

"Hocus-pocus," he said.

"Hocus-pocus?" I asked.

"Hocus-pocus," he insisted, and with that, he spun around and dropped the cards onto the kitchen table. The cards bounced, cartwheeled, and landed facedown. All except (yes, you've got it!) the seven of spades.

I was amazed. "How did you do that?" I asked. "That was awesome."

Andrew smiled and gathered up the cards. "That's for me

2. See Appendix 3 for some of the card tricks mentioned in this book.

to know and for you to find out," he said. "But not from me. A magician only shares his wisdom with other magicians."

"How do you know I'm *not* a magician?" I asked.

Andrew considered this. "I don't," he said, and put his cards back into the front pocket of his overalls. The magic show was over.

"Now," Andrew said as he took the pizza out of the oven and started sawing it in pieces, "tell me about Drew Hardy."

"How about after popcorn?" I said brightly. "I always make popcorn with my babysitters. For a snack."

"You're stalling," he said. "We haven't even eaten dinner."

"It's not polite to eat and talk at the same time," I tried. "Also, it's a long story."

"Your parents said they'd be back around eleven," he said. "When is your bedtime, anyway?"

"Ten," I said, which was stretching it. It's really nine-thirty, but if Mom and Dad didn't tell him before they left, then, technically, doesn't that mean that official bedtime has been canceled?

We both took bites of our pizza, and though my eyes were focused tightly on my plate, I knew Andrew was staring at me without blinking, which is something magicians, even ones that play shortstop for the Krieger Cats, are good at.

"Drew Hardy," I began, "is actually a friend of mine. Well, not exactly a friend of mine, because Drew Hardy is made up, but the person who made him up is my best friend, Carla Smith. You probably know one of her parents. She has four."

"Four what?"

"I just said," I said. "Parents. She has four parents." I proceeded to name them all—both Janices (or Januszes), Cliff, and Judy.

Andrew turned his baseball cap around so that the bill was touching his neck. That's what Andrew does when he's thinking hard. And when things get really intense, he takes the cap off and chews on it. Yes, chews on it. The bill is all frayed.

"I've had three of them," he said. "Not Cliff Smith. He's the only one. I was thinking of taking his poisonous snakes and frogs class next semester."

"Sounds . . . great," I said. Though I meant to sound doubtful, Andrew didn't seem to notice.

"I know," he said, turning his cap back the regular way.

"So is that your major?" I asked. "Biology?" (Hint: When you are talking to college students you've just met, it's always a good conversation starter to ask what they're majoring in.)

"No," he said. "I was thinking about double majoring, but I'm just a physics major."

"I know what you mean about 'just,' " I said. "I mean, Marie Curie won a Nobel Prize for chemistry *and* one for physics," I added casually, trying to impress him with my wealth of knowledge about physics (which, for your information, began and ended right there).

"Yeah," Andrew said, suddenly looking anxious and unhappy. (Hint: Be careful when asking college students about their major. It can make them very nervous—as in "Did I

32

make the right choice?" "Will I be able to get a job when I graduate?" and so on.)

"So Carla Smith is Drew Hardy," he said, changing the subject and the direction of his cap at the same time. "How come?"

I proceeded to tell him about *Harriet the Spy*—which, believe it or not, he not only had never read, but had never even heard of—and about how Carla wanted to be a spy or a private eye, not just when she grew up, which was too far in the future to be of much use, but right now, and how she thought that Drew Hardy had better name recognition than Carla Smith, even though a lot of people on campus know exactly who Carla Smith is, or at least who her parents are, and what they do, and where they live.

"I still don't get it," Andrew said. "What's so great about Drew Hardy? Aside from the fact that it's my nickname."

"It's a name recognition thing. Drew for Nancy Drew and Hardy for the Hardy Boys," I said.

"Oh," he said. "I get it. That's pretty smart. But does Carla really think anyone is going to hire you guys, especially when they see how old you are?"

He had a point. Who was going to hire two eleven-year-olds to solve mysteries that they couldn't solve themselves?

"Well, we're real cheap," I said. "You're not going to find a cheaper detective agency than ours. That should help. Anyway, look at you. *You* called."

"That's different," Andrew said.

"Well, it doesn't have to be."

6

We played blackjack for the rest of the night, and I didn't stand a chance. Andrew has some kind of super-memory thing: he can remember which cards have been shown and which are still in the deck. My mother should study *his* brain instead of the disgusting ones she picks at in her laboratory.

"Your mother is cool," Andrew said when I told him this.

"My mother is cool?" I repeated without conviction.

Andrew laughed. "You're probably too young to appreciate her."

Too young to appreciate my very own mother? Give me a break. I hate the way college students sometimes think they are so old and wise when, really, they are just high school kids once or twice removed. Last year there was this senior, Lily Chen-Danto, who was always saying stuff like "Oh, Sasha, your braids look adorable today. I wore my hair the exact same way when I was your age." *When I was your age.* I hate that, too.

"I appreciate my mother," I said, making sure he understood that I was offended.

Andrew laughed again. "Of course you do," he said. "That's not what I meant." He looked at his cards. "Hit me," he said.

I looked up at him to see if he was really serious. He nodded toward my hand.

"Oh," I said, "you want another card. I get it." I was embarrassed. Of course he didn't want me to hit him.

I dealt him another card.

"Blackjack," he said, laying out two jacks and an ace. "You sure you want to keep playing?"

I didn't answer. Not directly. I was still a little annoyed with him. "What about your mother," I growled at him. "Did you appreciate her when you were my age?"

"I never knew my mother," he said, dealing out another round.

"You never knew your mother? Ever?"

"Not my actual biological mother, no. I was adopted."

"Wow," I said.

Andrew turned his cap around. "Is that a good wow, or a bad wow?" he asked.

"Good—I guess," I said, but I wasn't sure. You know how in *The Secret Garden*, when Mary Lennox first gets sent to her uncle's house, you think it is the worst thing in the world?

But if you get to the end of the book, you think it was so perfect that she ended up there—for her, and for her cousin Colin, and especially for her uncle.

I must have been quiet for a long time because after a while Andrew rapped his knuckles on the table and said, "Hello? Are we playing cards here?"

"Sorry," I said. "I was thinking. Hit me."

Andrew handed me an eight of hearts.

"You know what I don't understand," I said later, when we were having a snack (not popcorn, but milk and graham crackers, because Andrew said he liked that better). "Why aren't there any regular families anymore? I mean, look at Carla. Look at you."

Andrew dipped his graham cracker into his milk, then took a bite. "Well, look at you. You live with both your parents. They're married to each other. That's pretty normal."

"Normal?" I said, dipping my own graham cracker into my own glass of milk. I was glad Mom had gotten the regular grahams and not the ones with cinnamon and sugar. I would not want to look down at those little grains of what look like sand floating in my milk. "I don't think so. We've got Danny."

That was when I told Andrew about my older brother and his problems, and about Trannell Academy, and the fact that one or the other of my parents has to go there every other weekend, and that I go, too, sometimes, and how, because of Danny, we had to sell our house and move into the dorm, and how I have to go to the Eraser twice a month—the whole en-chilada, as Carla's father, Cliff, likes to say when he means every single possible thing. Andrew listened carefully, moving his cap from front to back, and then he took it off and put it in his mouth. I took this as a good sign. I don't know about you, but I can usually tell who is going to be sympathetic and who is going to be a jerk. On the other hand, the Eraser is pretty much sympathetic—that's his job—but I still think he's a jerk. (Note to readers: Andrew Hardy is not at all like the Eraser.)

Just then there was a knock at the door, and it was a sophomore from the second floor who needed a lightbulb because she had accidentally tripped over the cord of her desk lamp, which had crashed to the floor. Andrew went upstairs with her to help her screw it in (which, if you ask me, is pretty lame—I mean, who can't screw in her own lightbulb?), and I was kind of annoyed because I had just spilled my guts and he was leaving. Also, it was getting late, and I was pretty sure he wouldn't have noticed this fact if the lamp-tripper had not interrupted us. I just knew when he came back he was going to tell me it was bedtime, and that would be that.

But that's not what happened. Andrew came back and sat down at the kitchen table again and continued chewing on his cap as if he had never left.

"I see what you mean about normal," he said after a while. "Maybe there really is no such thing as normal. Maybe normal is a myth."

"A myth?" I said. King Midas was a myth. Pandora was a myth. But the Abramowitz family? We are definitely not a myth.

"What I mean," Andrew said, "is that maybe we all have this idea of what's normal, but really what's normal is that every family is different.

"Let me ask you something," he said. "Have you ever heard of the boat people?"

I shook my head.

"They were people who tried to escape from Vietnam by building these boats—they were really more like rafts most of the time—and going out to sea, and hoping someone would find them. Most of them died. My mother, the one who adopted me, was a boat person. She was really little when she left Vietnam. She was one of the few people on her boat to survive. She was adopted by a family in Minnesota. A 'normal' American family, except for her. She made them different. But at the same time, they sort of made her normal, if you see what I mean."

"Wait a minute," I said. "I'm confused. Your mother was adopted, and *you* were adopted?"

"I was adopted *because* my mother was adopted," Andrew said. Then, seeing I was completely, utterly, totally lost, he smiled, and went on. "My mother and father, the ones that adopted me, already had four kids when they found out about me. They didn't have much money—Dad works on truck engines and Mom is a nurse's aide—but I guess Mom was like 'Hey, what would have happened to me if the Horslees hadn't taken me in?' and decided they could do it. Mom says it's her way of thanking the people who adopted her. I mean, they could barely afford to have me. That's why I was so worried about the Drew Hardy thing. I was counting on that money. I really need it. I try not to ask my parents for anything."

Just then the phone rang. When my parents are out they always check in between nine-thirty and ten, and the clock on the wall said they were right on time.

"Yes," Andrew said. "Yes. Yes, she is. Thanks," and hung up.

"I just told your parents that you had gone to bed," Andrew said, turning to me. "I guess you'd better not make a liar out of me."

I took a last sip of milk and grinned. But truthfully, underneath, I wasn't smiling at all. We had learned about refugees in social studies—about how in wartime people often have to leave their homes and start all over, and how they usually don't have anything—no clothes, except what they are wearing, no money, no place to live, no jobs. Sometimes they are so poor they have to eat bugs and tree bark. (I may be making this up, but I think I read it somewhere.)

"Well, good night, then," I said to Andrew. And because I guess I'm just used to it, I put my arms around his middle and gave him a hug. I think he was kind of surprised, because instead of hugging me back, he ruffled the top of my head, like I was a dog.

"Good night, Sasha," he said. I waved, and started walking down the hall.

"Hey, Sasha," Andrew said right before I turned in to the bathroom. "You're all right. Even if you did steal my name."

"That Andrew Hardy is some ballplayer," my dad said over the *Krieger Courier* at breakfast a couple of days later. "Listen to these statistics," and then he reeled off a bunch of numbers that meant nothing to me. "He's almost as good as Nomar." Nomar (whose name is really Ramon, if you look at it in the mirror) is one of my dad's favorite players. He used to be a Boston Red Sock. The Red Sox are one of my father's favorite teams. Their history, according to him, is "deeply, deeply tragic."

"You know what I heard," Dad continued. "I heard that Hardy was recruited by the University of Arizona, but that he decided to come here because he wanted a Krieger education."

Oh no. How many times had I heard those words, "a Krieger education"? I couldn't even begin to count. People here seem to think that Krieger is the only place in the world to go to college. They call it "Krieger pride," which is kind of a pun because the Krieger mascot is a lion, and lions travel in groups called prides.

But I have to admit, it is a really nice place. All the college buildings are set up on a grassy hill, and they are covered in ivy, which makes them look very old. One side of the hill faces the town, and the other side slopes down to farms and pastures and a big reservoir that becomes the college skating pond in the winter.

"Andrew is from Arizona," I informed my dad. "Tucson." (Note: Mrs. Blank never gives us proper nouns for spelling words but I think she should make an exception for Tucson. Who has ever heard of a silent "C"? [Okay, don't be funny. Obviously you can't hear a silent "C."])

"There's a game this afternoon against Jackson," Dad said. "Want to go?"

Ordinarily, this would not be my first choice for an after-school activity, but I wanted to see Andrew again and I wanted to see him play baseball, so I said, "Sure."

My father looked surprised but pleased.

"Do you want to come, too, dear?" he said, turning to Mom. "We can make it a whole family thing. You know, 'The Abramowitzes Go to the Ball Game.' "

I may have been imagining this, but I think I saw my mother shudder. I knew what she was thinking: "The *whole* family? What about Danny?"

"Can't," she said. "Today's the day we're doing PET scans."

I looked over at Tripod, snoozing comfortably on her big round red plaid bed, unaware that in just a few hours she would be part of one of my mother's experiments. Poor girl.

"Is this for Frank's project?" I asked hopefully.

"Which project is that, honey?" Mom asked absently.

"You know," I insisted. "Tripod's fourth leg."

My mother took a bite of the bagel she had every morning. (No, wise guy, not the same exact bagel every morning.)

"That's Deeprak Singh's course," she said when she finished chewing. "He teaches biomechanical engineering."

"Then whose pet are you working on?" I demanded.

"Why do you think I'm working on anyone's pet, Sasha?" my mother asked, taking another bite.

I have to say, I was pretty mad at her right then, and frustrated. First she says she's doing pet scans, then she pretends there's no pets involved.

"Jeez," I said. "Mom. You just said you were doing pet scans, didn't you?"

"Cool it, Sasha," my father said. "There's no reason to be mad at your mother."

"But—" I said.

My mother held up her hand like a traffic cop. "It's okay, Barney," she said. And then, turning to me, she said, "It's no one's pet, Sasha. 'P-E-T' stands for positron-emission tomography. It's a new way of taking pictures of the brain."

"Oh," I said. "Why didn't you tell me?"

"I just did," she said.

The game was down at Twin Park, so named for a pair of brothers—Morris and Sanford Parker—identical twins who graduated from Krieger during the Depression and later made a ton of money selling cars, some of which (the money, not the cars) they gave back to the college for the ball field. Daddy was already there when Carla and I rode up on our bikes. If you happen to be wondering why or how Carla was there, too, just keep in mind something that Daddy used to say all the time but doesn't anymore because it's so obvious: "Where's there's a Sasha, there's a Carla." He said it was a play on the phrase "Where there's a will, there's a way," which I never completely understood. Whatever. Carla and I are like glue. Two sides of the same coin, only my side is sturdy and dark, and her side is small and blond and wears glasses. (Warning: Do not under any circumstances—I repeat, do not, under any circumstances, ever call Carla Smith a runt. *You have been warned.*)

The two teams were warming up, and it was impossible to tell which player was Andrew, since all of our guys were in blue and had facial hair and all of their guys were in green, which made them look like giant blades of grass. But then Andrew noticed us and waved, and I saw that he was number eleven. Cat's eyes. Two ones. His lucky number, I supposed, although winning a Krieger baseball game would take more than luck. It would take a miracle.

This game was no different. They were up first; we were up second. They hit a home run in the third inning. We (meaning Andrew) hit a double in the bottom of the third and then were stranded at second base while the next three batters struck out. By the time the game had ended, Andrew had gotten three hits, none of them homers, and the Cats had exactly zero runs. It was depressing for everyone but my father. He found it "moving" and quoted a line from a poem by a poet I had never heard of. (Remember, I've probably heard of more poets than you have, since my father is a poet and his friends are poets and their friends are poets. Maybe your dad is a tree surgeon. You probably know more about trees than your average eleven-year-old.)

When it was all over, Andrew came up to us and said, "Hi, Sasha" to me, "Hello, Professor Abramowitz" to Dad, and then looked over at Carla and said, "Drew Hardy, I presume," and stuck out his dirty, sweaty hand. What choice did Carla have but to take it, though I knew, looking at her face, that she was not thrilled. "Solve any big cases yet?" he added. Carla shook her head and reddened. "No," she said quietly.

"Maybe she can figure out why the Krieger Cats never win a game," I said meanly, shooting Andrew an angry look. I hate it when people make fun of kids and make us feel like idiots.

"Good idea," Andrew said. "And when she does, maybe she can tell the coach. He's been scratching his head for seven years."

Then my father, who I'm sure had no idea what any of us were talking about, said, "Let's get ice cream," and the four of us walked up the hill to the Krieger snack bar, the Sugar Shack. Daddy and Andrew talked about the game and Carla and I talked about Andrew (she was much less mad at him than I was, just a little embarrassed), and even though no words were said about it, a general truce between Carla and Andrew and Andrew and me was declared.

8

Fact: If it's around ten in the morning on the second Sunday of the month, you will find me in one of my parents' cars (probably my mother's blue Honda Accord, which is more comfortable than my father's blue Honda Accord because the backseat of my father's car is strewn with books and papers and disgusting containers of moldy old food and broken umbrellas and boots and . . . I could go on). We are somewhere in the Berkshire mountains, which are more like tall, round hills than tall, rocky peaks, driving to West Stockbridge, where Danny goes to school. The second Sunday is always family day at Trannell, when the whole family is supposed to visit, not just the parents alone. They try to make it fun, with games and activities (like the time they had a clown who could stand on his head and walk on his hands), but it is never fun, not really, not the way the real circus is fun, even though when people ask you if you're having a good time you always say yes.

Fact: If you didn't know what it was, you'd probably think Trannell Academy was a regular school. The buildings are brick and they've got ivy creeping up the sides, just like at Krieger. There are dorms and a dining hall and a classroom building, a library, a gym. When it was first built, Trannell was a seminary that trained ministers. That was in the early 1800s. (Note: Isn't it strange how the 1800s are called the nineteenth century, and the 1900s are called the twentieth century? It's like your birthday. By the time you're ten, you're actually in your eleventh year, not that anyone ever tells you this. Instead they say things like "The reason you can't stay home alone is that you're too young. You're only ten, after all.") Then, during the Civil War, Trannell went out of business, since so many men who would have become ministers went off to war and got killed and there was no one to go to school there anymore. Then it became a girls' school, then an orphanage, then it kind of became an orphan itself, and was abandoned and boarded up. I'm not sure when that was.

Fact: There's this ancient photograph of twenty girls in identical long-sleeve, high-neck dresses with hats in their laps and their hands folded on top of the hats that says TRANNELL ACADEMY FOR YOUNG WOMEN, 1889 hanging in the Trannell library. Sometimes I like to think that maybe some of their great-great-great-great-grandchildren go to Trannell now. You never know. Anyone can have "problems."

Fact: This is what scares me.

So it was Sunday morning, right around ten, and we had just passed the old train depot that is now the Kobe Japanese Steakhouse Grill, and the True Value hardware store, and the village post office. Our car was behind a car from New York and in front of one from Maine, and I supposed they were heading up the hill to Trannell, too. But then the car in front turned right and we kept going straight, and then the other car peeled away left and we were alone, just me and Mom and Dad, driving on Route 61, not saying a word.

"I wonder if he's grown some more," my mother said after a while. Apparently Danny was going through a growth spurt. That's what his counselor had said. (Fact: At Trannell, the teachers are called counselors, like at camp.) "See if you notice, Sasha," she said to me—meaning, I guess, that since I hadn't seen Danny in a month, I might notice more of a change than she or Dad would, since they were just here two weeks ago. I didn't say anything.

Soon the tops of the Trannell buildings came into view, and after that, the fence. It's made of black iron and wraps around the whole campus. The only way in and out of Trannell is through the front gate, unless you want to climb the fence, which I would not recommend, since there are spikes at the top. The gate is guarded by men in blue uniforms who look like real policemen even though they're not. They couldn't arrest you, for example, if they saw you weren't wearing your seat belt.

My seat belt was still on when we pulled up at the gatehouse. So, I noticed, were Mom and Dad's. I think they find it hard to come here, even though they do it all the time. Usually Daddy leans out the window, shows his weekend visitor's pass, shows his driver's license, explains who we are and who we are visiting, and only then is allowed to drive up the hill. That's if Jack Starling isn't working. Mr. Starling has seen us here so many times that he just waves us through.

This time Mr. Starling held his hand up, but didn't wave. Daddy slowed and opened his window.

"Hi, Jack," he said. "What's up?"

Mr. Starling pointed to the wide Trannell lawn. "I just saw your Danny over there," he said. "With Pennypacker." Mr. Starling always talks like that. He says "your Danny," as if we might have forgotten exactly who Danny belonged to, as if he were a pair of mittens we could lose, or a house we owned, or a book. ("Your book is in the car." "You left your mittens on the bus." "Your Danny is over there, walking with Pennypacker.")

John Pennypacker is Danny's counselor. He is an older man with a shaved head and a pair of half-glasses that perch at the end of a particularly long nose. Before he was at Trannell, Penny—almost everyone calls him Penny—was a Marine.

We saw them walking between the trees—Penny, who is tall and thin and whose lack of hair makes him look even taller, and Danny, who is also tall, but not so thin. Penny had his arm around Danny's back.

"He looks agitated," my mother said.

Though "agitated" has never been an official school vocabulary word, I've been hearing it since the day I was born, and that's no exaggeration. Danny went from a baby who would lie on his back in his crib hour after hour, staring at a black-and-white Holstein cow mobile dangling from the ceiling, to someone who would say the same thing over and over and then go nuts if someone interrupted him. "He's agitated," one of my parents would say to the other then. Or "He's getting agitated." Or "Danny, calm down, you're about to be agitated." How could I not know the meaning of "agitated" after watching Danny get upset and hit and throw things and yell at my parents and at me and at Tripod. It wasn't all day. It wasn't every day. But it was a lot.

"It's okay to hate your brother sometimes," my doctor, the Eraser, said once, but I don't know. Is it, really?

9

Mrs. [Fill-in-the] Blank used to say that a good writer is like a good poker player—she never reveals her hand. But that was before one of the parents of a kid in our class complained to the principal that Mrs. Blank was using a "sinful card game to teach impressionable young children." Now Mrs. Blank says things like "Pretend your story is a birthday present and unwrap it slowly." Which is why I didn't explain the thing about Danny and the swimming pool earlier, I only mentioned it. You're supposed to have been thinking about it ever since and wondering if I'd bring it up again.

I was trying to build suspense. Mrs. Blank is obsessed with suspense the same way my father was obsessed with cleaning the pool. The pool had a blue bottom and blue sides, and because Dad had heard of a little baby swallowing dirty pool water and getting an infection and dying, and because he had a little baby (by the name of Sasha Marie Curie Abramowitz), he decided to do everything to keep that pool clean. He bought a vacuum cleaner that worked underwater and all sorts of pool brushes and pumps and chemicals. At least three times a week he skimmed the surface of the pool for dead bugs and leaves and scrubbed the sides and bottom with a special brush while the pump, which he had taken off and apart, was soaking in a solution of vinegar and hot water in our kitchen sink. Then he'd throw a combination of chemicals into the pool—one part this to two parts that—and tell my mother that it made him so happy, figuring out if the right formula was one part this to two parts that, or two parts that to three parts this, that he was thinking of hanging up his hat as a poet and becoming a chemist. "So to speak," he'd say, just so we'd understand that he didn't actually have a poetry hat the way, say, Mr. Starling, the Trannell guard, has a policeman's hat (though this was before we knew Mr. Starling). But he didn't become a chemist; he just wrote poems about it.

Danny loved the pool. He went out every day in the summer, even in the rain, and floated on his back with his eyes closed. Maybe he was pretending he was one of the leaves. Maybe he was just happy to be rid of the heaviness of his body. Whatever it was, it calmed him down. He was happy in the pool. He was himself in the pool.

My parents were happy, too. No, they were thrilled. Afterward they said they didn't really notice that Danny was spending more and more time in the pool. What they noticed was that he was spending less and less time upset and lashing out and saying the same thing over and over again and crying miserably and making me cry miserably and making them cry miserably.

Daddy drove slowly onto the school grounds, and when he heard the car, Penny turned, saw it was us, and waved. His arm was still around Danny's back, which was a good sign, because when my brother is really upset he won't let anyone touch him, not even Tripod.

That's what he was like that day in the pool. Danny got in at exactly 7:30 in the morning, before I was up and while my parents were reading the paper and drinking coffee and not completely paying attention. He slid into the pool (he never jumped—he was superstitious about jumping, like it would bring him bad luck) and then every minute and a half he'd flip over, back to front to back again. ("Flip like a burger?" I once asked Daddy. "No," he said. "Not *like* a burger. Not *like* anything I've ever seen or care to see again.") Ninety seconds on his back, ninety seconds on his stomach, ninety seconds on his back. It was like clockwork, only he wasn't wearing a watch.

"He's counting," Mom told Daddy as they watched from the kitchen window. "It's like he's a living second hand." I was up by then. The real clock said it was seventeen minutes after eight.

"Well, as long as he's not hurting anyone, let's let him be,"

Daddy said. He said he wanted to get to the barbershop to work on the poem he was writing. Mom said okay. She had a meeting that morning—her Tuesday lab conference with her summer assistants—so she had to leave, too. That left me, of course, and Danny, and Tripod, and our babysitter, Jenny Flum, a Krieger student who was living with us that summer and working as a mother's helper.

Jenny gave me breakfast and then told me I couldn't go in the pool for half an hour, otherwise I'd get cramps and die. I liked Jenny, but she was a theater major and could be very, shall we say, dramatic. Meanwhile, there was Danny, a minute and a half on one side, a minute and a half on the other, and I don't think anyone made him wait any thirty minutes before he went in the water or even checked to see if he'd eaten any breakfast. (Note: When Danny went to Trannell, Mom and Dad had to sign an agreement that said they would never, as long as he was there, bring him food—no cookies, no candy, no ice cream. They are very strict about food at Trannell. No Froot Loops or Honey Nut Cheerios. No gum. No Life Savers or Tic Tacs. Something about how sugar screws up your blood chemistry.)

Finally, after twenty-eight of the required thirty minutes, I went to my room to put on my bathing suit. (Note to Mom: Even though it was almost four years ago I still remember which one. It was the two-piece blue one with the black dolphins that you got for me from L.L. Bean. Isn't it funny how people remember details from certain days and not from others?) Jenny also put on her suit, and we got towels and sunscreen and went outside. It was a regular summer's day, sunny and getting hot. It was great to have a pool right out the back door.

So out the back door we went, and there was Danny, still flipping and flopping. His bathing suit was blue, too, and baggy. It would fill with water every time he'd turn, and look like a balloon.

"Hi, Danny," Jenny called. No response. Just the swish of water, flip and flop.

Not that this was unusual, especially not that summer, and especially not when Danny was in the pool. Most of the time it seemed as if he didn't notice anything but whatever he was doing. In this case, flipping and flopping.

Jenny went in the water first. Or was about to.

"*Stop!*" Danny shrieked. "*Stop! Do not move! Do not come in here! You cannot come in here!*" He was shouting as loudly as he could.

Jenny pulled her foot back from the ladder. "What's the matter, Danny?" she asked. "You scared me." I looked at her face. It didn't look scared. But you never knew. She wanted to be an actress on Broadway when she graduated, and was always trying out faces. (She could cry just by thinking about crying.)

Danny didn't respond.

"Danny?"

No response.

"We're coming in, then, Danny," Jenny said. Her jaw was set and her brow was furrowed. She looked mad. This looked like real mad, not acting mad. "We're coming in," she tried again. "Me and Sasha."

"Bacteria!" my brother yelled. *"Bacteria. Contamination. Die, die, die."* He scrambled out of the pool and before we knew what he was doing he was swinging the pail with chlorine in it, the one that said POISON and FLAMMABLE and KEEP OUT OF REACH OF CHILDREN in big black letters. He pulled the lid off and tossed it aside and pulled out the little shovel my father used to measure how much chlorine to put in the water.

"Bacteria!" Danny yelled again, and came toward us with the pail rocking back and forth, pointing the shovel, full of white stuff, at us like a gun.

"Stop it, Danny," Jenny said.

"Bacteria, bacteria, bacteria, bacteria," my brother said, plus a bunch of completely unprintable words.

"Put that down right now," Jenny said. And then, to me, "Go inside, Sasha."

"No," I said.

"Go inside." Jenny's voice was tight and mad, and when I looked at her face I saw that she had tears in her eyes. Real (not acting) tears.

Danny, meanwhile, continued to shout *"Bacteria!"* and curses, and wave the little shovel full of poison.

I went inside. Even though I hadn't been in the water yet, I was freezing. In preschool they taught us to dial 911 in case

57

of an emergency, but I was completely confused. Was this an emergency? I didn't know. As I stood there I saw our neighbor, Mrs. Mendelsohn, who is old and hard of hearing, getting into her yellow Lincoln Town Car and suddenly I knew what to do. I ran out the front door, calling her name. I guess her hearing aid was working just fine because she stopped halfway down her driveway and rolled down her window. I didn't even let her say hello.

"Mrs. Mendelsohn," I said quickly, "something is happening with Danny, he thinks we're bacteria, and we've got to stop him."

"What's that, dearie?" she said. She called everyone dearie. "Danny's caught some bacteria?" On second thought, maybe her hearing aid wasn't working that well.

"No," I insisted. "It's Danny. He's—" But what was he? Upset? Angry? Crazy?

"What would you like me to do, dearie?" Mrs. Mendelsohn said. "I'm already late for the hairdresser's. I'm down for a perm *and* highlights."

I could still hear Danny shouting, and Jenny shouting, and now Mrs. Mendelsohn was starting up her engine again, which almost drowned them out. Suddenly, inspired, I guess, by the words "perm" and "highlights," I said, "Could you please drop me off at the barbershop?" and hopped in the backseat before she could say no.

"Yes, you could use a trim, dearie," she said, looking me

over in the rearview mirror. A horn honked. We had almost backed into the college shuttle bus.

Say what you will about little old ladies in general, or Mrs. Mendelsohn in particular, but she drove so fast I was sure we were going to get stopped for speeding. And I'm not convinced anyone had ever told her the meaning of yellow and red traffic lights. We were at the barbershop in no time. I got out and she pulled away before I could even say goodbye.

It was only then, standing on the sidewalk of the main street in Krieger, that I realized I had nothing on. Not nothing completely, but almost nothing completely—just my two-piece dolphin bathing suit, and sandals. Oh my God, I was *not going* to go through that door.

Luckily for me, I guess, Gus Barnes, the barber, saw me standing there and must have said something to my father, because a minute later there he was, pen behind his ear, coming toward me. My feet didn't move, but my body began to shake. Shake and shake, and then I was crying and Daddy was holding me and saying "What's wrong? What's wrong?" and I couldn't speak. "Danny," I managed to say, and without waiting to hear more, my father lifted me up and started to run toward his car, which was parked around the back.

"Tell me, Sasha," he said when we were driving home, and I did.

I think he meant to tell me to stay in the car when we reached our house, but he forgot, which was a good thing because he also forgot to put on the emergency brake, and about ten minutes later the car rolled down the driveway into a hemlock tree, smashing the parking lights and putting a dent in the bumper. Danny was back in the pool, doing his ninety-second flips. Jenny Flum was in the house, on the phone. Her eyes and nose were red from crying. She was talking to her mom.

"Yes, this evening, the 5:27 bus. It goes through Springfield. I should be there around midnight. No, it's fine. The bus is fine. No, you don't have to come get me."

So that was settled. Jenny Flum was leaving. She hung up the phone.

"I'm going, Professor Abramowitz," she said to Daddy in a deep, almost stern voice. I knew that voice. It was one of her made-up ones.

"I understand, Jenny," Daddy said, distracted, looking through the window at Danny in the pool.

"You understand?" Jenny said. She sounded furious. "You understand?" And then she burst out crying, too, and Daddy had to put his arms around her, the way he had with me, until she could calm down enough to talk again. It was at that very moment that the car crashed, and Daddy swore and slapped his hands against his thighs and looked like he was going to cry, too.

"Did you call Professor Abramowitz?" Daddy asked Jenny after a while.

"I left her a message," she said, and started to sob again. "I didn't know where you were!" she said, looking at me. "I thought you had run away."

For some reason, watching Jenny weep over me made me cry again, too, and we both stood there, with tears overflowing our eyes, and then Jenny held out her arms, and I gave her a hug, or maybe she gave me a hug, I'm not sure who started it, but by the time it was finished, Daddy had left the room and was by the pool, talking to Danny.

"Get out right now," I heard him say. "I need you to come out right now." Danny didn't say a word.

Daddy started up the steps to the deck of the pool, but he never got to the top rung.

"Bacteria!" Danny shouted. "Parasite."

"Out of the pool. Now," Daddy said. Talk about stern voices. But then Daddy stopped, and said, "Oh holy God in heaven," which is his way of not saying something worse. Danny had taken all the pool chemicals, not just the pail of chlorine he had been swinging at me and Jenny, but all of them, both forty-pound sacks that Daddy had bought on sale when the pool store in Krieger went out of business, and made a big mountain of them at the entrance to the pool. Daddy would have to wade through it to reach Danny, and risk getting chemical burns.

Daddy went back down the steps and walked toward the garage. He did not look angry, just tired and old. In a minute he was back, with a snow shovel. Danny was waiting for him.

"Bacteria," he said, and then the bad words. "Stop!" he

screamed as Daddy bent over to clear a path through the chemicals. We heard him say something to Daddy, low, and Daddy say something to him. We couldn't make it out. Then we heard Danny say the word "flammable." Then the word "explosion." Then the words "eliminate the bacteria."

"Let me get this straight," my father said to my brother. Loudly, for our benefit, I thought. "You think I am bacteria. You think bacteria must be eliminated. You are going to make this chlorine explode if I come nearer. You are going to pee on it."

Ordinarily I might think that someone threatening to make something explode by peeing on it was completely hilarious, but I knew from all of Daddy's lectures on pool safety that this was no empty threat. How many times had he said "Chlorine plus urine equals disaster!"?

Daddy came inside then, and went into his bedroom and shut the door. Jenny went up to her room to pack, and I went to mine to change, then went across the hall to Jenny's and watched from the doorway as she opened drawers and tossed clothes into a big black duffel bag, not even trying to keep things folded or neat. She put in her books and photographs, too, then stripped the bed and piled the sheets in the corner.

"Do you think your parents will mind if I leave these here?" she asked.

I shrugged. "I doubt it," I said. "What are you going to do now? I mean, for the rest of the summer?"

Jenny shook her head. "I don't know," she said. "I've got this internship at the National Theatre of the Deaf, but that's not till September." She sounded distant, like she was already gone.

I went in and lay down on the mattress in her room. Maybe I'd ask Mom if I could trade and have this room and make my room the one for guests. Mine was bigger, but this one had a skylight, which was sending a warm beam of light across my legs.

Just then my father popped his head in and told me I was leaving. "It's all arranged," he said. "Janusz is waiting downstairs."

"Janusz?" I said.

"Janusz," he said, and handed me a knapsack. My knapsack, the violet one I used to have, with my monogram on the pocket in block letters.

"But Carla is away," I said. "She's at horse camp."

"Say goodbye to Jenny," Daddy said. Clearly he wasn't interested in discussing the details.

Confession: When I was younger I was scared of Janusz. Even though he was my best friend's stepfather, I thought he was frightening. He had a thick accent (think: Count Dracula) and nose hair and long, bony fingers. Because he let me sit up in the front seat that day, I got to stare at those fingers the whole way over to Carla's house.

"I don't see why I have to leave," I said as we backed out of the driveway, past my father's Honda, which was still leaning against the tree it had crashed into. "It's unfair."

Janusz took his right hand off the steering wheel and rubbed his chin. I thought he was going to say something, but he didn't. (That's another reason Janusz used to scare me. He doesn't say much. It used to make me nervous. I'm used to it now. Also, he rarely uses the words "the," "a," and "an" when he talks.)

One second later, Janusz slammed on the brakes. We both lurched forward and then snapped back like pieces of elastic.

"What was that?" he asked, turning to stare at the yellow Lincoln that had cut us off.

"That," I said, "was Mrs. Mendelsohn."

"She is lunatic," Janusz said under his breath.

"She's okay," I said, remembering our ride that morning. Then, without thinking, I craned my neck so I could see my face in the rearview mirror. Mrs. Mendelsohn said I needed a haircut. Did I?

"It is lunch," Janusz said, as we drove past the clock outside the National Bank of Krieger. The clock said it was 12:36, and though I hadn't noticed it before, I was hungry. (Note to the Eraser: Was that a *real* feeling, or something I made up because I thought, since it was around noon, that I was *supposed* to be hungry?) "You want burger?"

"Okay," I said. This was before I became a vegetarian, when I still ate things like roast beef sandwiches and hamburgers and hot dogs.

Janusz stopped the car in front of the Diner on Main and we got out. Ordinarily the place was packed with students taking a break from the Krieger Commons cafeteria, but since it was summer the place was pretty empty.

"Can we sit at the counter?" I asked. Janusz looked relieved. This way we'd only have to look at the pies in the display case, not at each other. We ordered club burgers and ginger ales, and before they came a man who recognized Janusz sat down beside him and started to ask him about Venus, and which other planets would be visible that month, and telling him about a new camera he wanted to get so he would be able to take pictures of stars, and then I lost track of what they were talking about because I was thinking of Danny, back in the pool, and Daddy trying to get him out, and suddenly I knew I was going to be sick, very, very sick, and I had to get out of there before I did you-know-what all over everything, and I don't know how, but the counter waitress seemed to know exactly what was going on, because she came over and didn't even ask, she just took me by the elbow and we got to the employees' washroom right around the same time that everything I had eaten that day and the day before and the day before that and possibly forever came rushing out of my stomach as if someone were in there yelling *"Fire! Fire!"*

"Sasha? Are you all right?" That was Janusz, on the other side of the door.

"It's okay," said the waitress, whose tag told me her name was Terri. "Just give her a minute."

I smiled at her weakly and wiped my face with a paper towel and wondered if she realized she was lying. *It* was not okay. And it would be way more than one minute before *it* ever was.

10

Danny broke free of Penny and came over to Daddy's side of the car. "What did you bring me?" Danny demanded, and Daddy was just about to speak when Mr. Pennypacker, who was right behind him, said "Danny!" sharply, and gave him a knowing look.

"Yeah right hi how are you it's nice to see you I'm good," Danny said, hardly separating one syllable from the next, and in the tone of voice that makes Mrs. Blank tug on her hair in reading group and moan, "More expression, thank you."

But Penny didn't seem to care about expression. "Good, Danny," he said, keeping his eyes fixed on Danny, who scowled and said something nasty under his breath and then, louder, "What did you bring?"

Daddy slipped his hand into his shirt pocket and pulled out three baseball cards, which he handed over to my brother.

Danny studied each one carefully, and for a long time. He grunted. Danny, like Daddy, is a baseball fanatic. But, unlike Daddy, Danny can reel off whole rosters from any year and tell you who hit grand slams on which days, and what the temperature and wind speed were that afternoon, and what time the sun set. Mom says he has "that kind" of memory, but she never says what kind "that kind" is.

Danny shuffled the cards. I knew there was a Gary Carter World Series Championship card from 1986, a Pete Rose rookie card, and a vintage Carl Yastrzemski. "Yaz" played for the Red Sox in the sixties, and Daddy always tries to include at least one Red Sox card. "The Red Sox teach us the meaning of patience," Daddy likes to say. (Fact: Patience is something Danny could use.)

Daddy looked over at Penny. "Okay?" he asked.

Penny nodded.

Daddy said, "They're yours," to Danny. Not that Danny noticed. In his mind they were his already.

But that was the ritual. Daddy would bring the cards, Danny would look at the cards, Penny would decide if Danny could have the cards—based on whether he'd been good or not—and then Daddy would tell Danny the cards were his—a reward for good behavior. Penny called it "behavior modification." He said that Danny could be "trained" to behave the right way. And it seemed to be working. He was calmer, less agitated. There was even talk of sending him home for a few weeks in the summer, though that's what they always said, and it never happened. (Fact: If I said one one-hundreth of the bad words that come tumbling out of Danny's mouth, I'd be grounded for life and fed bread and water through a little slot in my bedroom window. But Danny can't help it. It's part of what's wrong with him. In the immortal words of the Eraser: "That's his illness talking, Sasha.")

While Danny was examining the cards, we found a place to park. Then Danny and Penny came over to the car again and Mom and Dad and I each hugged Danny, who just stood there, as usual, and let us. He never hugs back. It's like he can't.

"You've grown," I said to Danny. (Fact: People are always saying this to me. Fact: I hate it.)

"Yes," all the adults agreed, and then Danny and my dad, and Penny and my mom, paired off up the path, leaving me to trail behind them. This is the way it always is on "family" day. I pulled out a notebook and pen from my knapsack and started taking notes: "Danny, taller. Some facial hair. Red tulips along the garden path. Gary Carter, Pete Rose, Yaz." Daddy says the best writing has a lot of details. So does Mrs. Blank. (Fact: Her hooded eyes are the color of storm clouds.)

I used to just read during family day, sitting in the lounge or under a tree in the garden, but one time I heard Penny ask Mom if I often soothed myself with books, which made me mad. I wasn't "soothing" myself, I was trying to keep from having to talk to the other kids who have brothers or sisters like Danny—or worse. I mean, it's not like we have anything else in common. I would have said this, but I know it would have been reported back to the Eraser, and then we'd have to spend half an hour talking about it. Boring, boring, boring. I'd rather talk about Ted Williams, and how his kids decided to have him specially frozen when he died rather than burying him or having him cremated. (Fact: "Cremated" was not and never will be one of Mrs. Blank's vocabulary words. Look it up if you don't know what it means.)

"Do you think about death a lot, Sasha?" the Eraser asked when I just happened to mention that thing about Ted Williams. (Note: It didn't *mean* anything. I was just making small talk.)

"I don't know," I said. "What's a lot?"

That, by the way, is a trick that Carla, who had to see the Eraser for a year when her parents got divorced, taught me. Answer a question with a question, and the conversation may get sidetracked. But it doesn't always work, like when the Eraser said, "A lot is whatever you think is a lot, Sasha," which made me feel like a moron.

I said, "No, I don't think I think about death a lot," and the Eraser wrote that down. (Note to myself: Bring notebook to next session with Eraser. Write down everything *he* says.)

I had to see the Eraser the very next day. That's the schedule: visit Danny on a Sunday, see the Eraser after school on a Monday. I used to go with Mom and she would just sit there and pretend to grade papers, but now I go by myself. I walk to his office from school, check myself in, park myself in the big red easy chair by the window in his waiting room, read "Humor in Uniform" in the *Reader's Digest* or look for the hidden pictures in *Highlights* and wait for the receptionist to call out my name. That's the part I hate the most. Usually I like my name, but not when it's broadcast throughout the offices of Drs. Serkowsky, Galen, and Rainey. It's like there's someone with a microphone shouting, *"Attention, attention, attention, people. In case you haven't noticed, Sasha Abramowitz is here. Sasha Abramowitz is here to talk to Dr. Serkowsky about her feelings."* Give me a break.

"What's this?" the Eraser asked when I pulled my orange Garfield notebook and a blue pen out of my knapsack after sitting down in the corner of his worn leather couch where I always sit, rain or shine, every single time.

"What does it look like?" I wanted to say, but before I could, he sneezed, big-time. That's when I noticed his eyes were runny behind his glasses, and the tip of his nose and the skin around it were red.

"Spring colds are the worst," the Eraser said, reaching over to the table between us and taking a tissue from the box that was there, I always thought, for the patients. In case they got so sad that they cried—which, according to Carla, happened all the time there. (Once she walked into the supply closet, thinking it was the bathroom, and saw about a hundred boxes of tissues, the kind with lotion, so your nose doesn't get all raw like the Eraser's. I guess the lotion doesn't work.) Personally, I don't see why anyone would pay someone to make them cry, but then again I don't know why anyone would pay someone to ask what a notebook and pen is. Luckily, the sneeze distracted him and he didn't ask again. Instead he said, "So how did it go, Sasha?" which is pretty much what he says every time, except when he says something dopey about the weather like "Sure is windy today."

"Okay," I answered. I once made the mistake of saying "Okay, I guess," which caused the Eraser to raise his bushy eyebrows so high they sent ripples of skin up to his scalp like tidal waves, and then he made me talk about it till it was time to go. (Note: If you are ever curious about how someone can spend more than half an hour discussing the meaning of "I guess," make an appointment to see the Eraser.)

"How did Danny seem?" he asked.

"The same," I said. For some reason, saying this reminded me of when we have square dancing in gym, with the boys standing in a line opposite the girls and Mrs. Blank calling out instructions: "Bow to your partner, do-si-do your partner, swing your partner, change." What I mean is that our conversations are like scripts. The Eraser says what he is supposed to say. I say what I am supposed to say. He bows, I bow. He do-si-dos, I do-si-do. The difference is that nothing ever seems to change. Not me, not the Eraser, not Danny.

"Is that frustrating for you, Sasha?" the Eraser asked. Sometimes, I have to admit, it's like that man can read my mind.

"I don't know," I said. (Fact: This was both true and untrue. Isn't that weird, how the same thing can be true and false at the very same time? *Paradox, n., a self-contradictory statement that appears to be true.* Fact: Sometimes I am actually relieved when certain words appear on our vocabulary list and I learn that the way I am feeling or looking at things is so common that there's a word for it.)

I doodled in my notebook, then wrote down the stuff about the Eraser's cold, a description of his nose—red, raw, swollen. (Note: "Bulbous" would be a good vocabulary word. Suggest

73

this to Mrs. Blank. Also suggest a vocabulary word suggestion box. Extra credit?)

"What are you writing there?" the Eraser wanted to know. He had that tone of voice that's supposed to sound patient but instead sounds like someone pretending to be patient, which is supposed to tell you that he's not feeling patient at all.

"Notes," I said. "It's a school thing."

"Do you think it's a good idea to do homework during our time together?" the Eraser said. (Translation: I don't think it's a good idea at all.)

"It's not homework," I said.

"But you said—"

"My teacher, Mrs. Blank, says that the best books are full of details," I said.

The Eraser raised his eyebrows again but said nothing. This is one of his tricks—to look directly at me and say nothing and wait for something to pop out of my mouth out of nervousness. But not this time. I went back to my notebook.

"Are you hoping to write a book, Sasha?" the Eraser asked after a while.

"Yes," I said, and then regretted it instantly. I had just broken Rule #1 with the Eraser: Reveal nothing. Now we'd have to talk about it forever. Why did I want to write a book and would it be fiction or autobiography or a mystery and who were the main characters and what was the title, blah, blah, blah.

But the Eraser surprised me. He just nodded and smiled

and said, "I hear that Danny might be coming home this summer."

I gulped. How did he know that already? Had Mom or Daddy called? Was he in touch with Penny? I hate it when I think—no, when I *know* that things are going on behind my back. If things are going on behind my back, doesn't that mean they are bigger deals than I thought they were? Or didn't think? Because the truth is, even though my parents and Penny had all mentioned it, I hadn't really paid attention. Danny had come home before, for long weekends, and it had been all right—a little tense, but all right. And the absolute fact of the matter was that they had talked about him coming home for the summer every year and it never happened. But this—having the Eraser bring it up—this was serious.

"Earth to Sasha," the Eraser said, as if I might find that even a tiny bit funny. "Do you read me?"

"They say that every year," I said, clicking the top of my pen, in and out, in and out. I saw the Eraser write something down, probably about the pen. I kept on clicking it anyway. Then he blew his nose. (I wrote this down.) Then he said, "This year it might actually happen," while he was still wiping his nose.

"How come?" I asked.

"From what I understand, he seems to be doing well, and the new medication is working, so your parents and Mr. Pennypacker think it's a good idea."

"Oh," I said, which really meant "Oh no." Danny hasn't

lived with us, really, for years. He doesn't even have a real room in our campus apartment at Krieger, since he went to Trannell before we moved there. When he visits he sleeps in the study, which, even though it is decorated with Red Sox posters and pennants and is where my parents store the Ferris wheel Danny made from his Erector set when he was my age, doesn't count as an actual bedroom. The only place to put your clothes is a box underneath the bed, because there's no dresser and the closet is crammed with my parents' old lecture notes.

"A penny for your thoughts," the Eraser said, startling me. For a minute I had forgotten where I was. Now I remembered all too well: in the office of an annoying person with a runny nose who was pretending to offer me a penny to say what was on my mind.

"I was just thinking that there isn't really room for Danny," I said.

The Eraser wrote this down, then glanced at his watch. (I wrote down that the Eraser wrote this down, then glanced at his watch.)

"Our time is up, Sasha," he said, capping his pen, "but there is something I want you to think about."

I rolled my eyes, secretly, to myself. The Eraser was always sending me off with things to think about. Usually they were things I didn't want to think about at all, and probably wouldn't have, if he hadn't told me to think about them, which caused me to try *not* to think about them, which is exactly the same thing *as* thinking about them.

"When you say that there isn't really room for Danny," the Eraser went on, "do you mean in your house or in your family?

"It's a hard question," he said, showing me the door.

12

The next time I saw Andrew Hardy was at Pinky Summers's birthday party. Pinky (whose real name is Thaddeus) is a boy in my class who I've known practically since the second we moved to Krieger. I had an ear infection and he had an ear infection and our mothers met at the pediatrician's. (My ears cleared up, but his were so bad he had to get tubes put in them.) Our moms liked each other and just assumed we would like each other, which turned out to be true. This is because Pinky is not your average soccer-ball-kicking, karate-chopping, girl-hating boy. He's just a regular person who happened to be born in a boy's skin. At least, that's how I explain the fact that even when the other boys used to give him a hard time about being friends with me—not me, Sasha Abramowitz, but me, a *girl*—he didn't pay attention. It's not like they don't notice now, either, but they've just given up.

Pinky Summers is just who he is, take it or leave it. "Pinky Summers is a leader, not a follower," my parents like to say, which under other circumstances might make me want to throw up, but in this case does not. Pinky Summers has the Sasha Abramowitz seal of approval. It's not his fault that people like him.

"How do you know Andrew?" I whispered to Pinky when I handed him his present (a really cool whittling set with ten pieces of balsa wood and a silver-handled pocketknife) and noticed, over his shoulder, Andrew Hardy setting up in the Summerses' family room.

"I don't," he whispered back. "Someone in Mom's book group hired him for her kid's party and said he was great."

"Sweet," I said loudly, causing Andrew to look up from what he was doing—shuffling cards—and see that it was me. He nodded and smiled but didn't say a thing. At first I was a little hurt, but then I remembered that he had told me that before he played baseball or did card tricks or took a test he had to get into his "game head." So I didn't say anything to Andrew, either, I just watched him shuffle cards, practice routines in his head, and fiddle with his tie—white, in contrast to his black shirt, which I thought was a little tacky and not original enough, like he got it in a secondhand magician's clothing store. (Note: Remember to tell Andrew this, but in a polite way.) Then Mrs. Summers, who is a fantastic baker and, shall we say, a fairly rotund person (thank you, Mrs. Blank, for providing a word that means fat without having to actually say it, which would be rude), announced that there would be cupcakes and chocolate milk before the show, to be followed by ice cream cake and cookies after the show, and there was a general stampede into the Summerses' dining room, which left Andrew and me by ourselves.

"If you need an assistant. For your tricks . . ." I ventured.

"Oh, thanks," Andrew said. "I'm all set."

"Okay." Andrew's stubbly beard was a little longer than last time, but it was still patchy. He looked like the Wooly Willy toy I used to have, which let me "paint" a beard with slivers of metal on the face of a man who my father said looked like he had just escaped from jail. In Andrew's case, though, it was part of his Krieger Cats uniform. Every year the Cats take a public vow not to shave their beards until they win a game. And every year for the past seven years they've ended the season looking, Daddy says, like philosophers.

"How's business?" Andrew asked. He had stopped shuffling and was exercising his fingers by passing a quarter from knuckle to knuckle on one hand without touching it with the other.

"Business?"

"Drew Hardy and Associates," he said.

"Oh, that," I said. "I think we're out of business."

Andrew scowled. "So soon?"

"It was Carla's idea," I said. "She's always getting these ideas, like at least one a day. She gets really excited about them, and then I get really excited about them, and then she forgets about the idea from the day before because she's so into the new one, but I haven't. It can get a little frustrating." Why I was saying something negative about my best friend to Andrew Hardy, I do not know. All I know is that I didn't want Andrew to think that I was a quitter.

"So what is she on to now?" Andrew asked.

"Trash," I said.

"Trash? As in the stuff people throw away?"

"Exactly. Carla thinks that people—well, Americans— throw away things when they are still perfectly good just because they are tired of them. She hasn't decided what to do about it, though. Maybe collect it and send it to people in Kuala Lumpur."

"Kuala Lumpur?"

"I think she did a report about it once."

"Interesting," Andrew said. "So why don't you take it over, then?"

"Kuala Lumpur?" I asked.

"No. Drew Hardy and Associates, Private Investigators."

"I don't know. Like I said, it was Carla's idea. She's Drew Hardy."

"No," Andrew said, "I'm Drew Hardy."

Just then Mrs. Summers flicked the lights. *"Five minutes to showtime!"* she hollered. "Please find a seat." People started to trickle back into the room.

I sat right in the front where I could really watch Andrew

work. What was the point of taking over Drew Hardy and Associates if Drew Hardy and Associates never got any work? I wondered. What did Andrew have up his sleeve?

The ace of hearts, it turned out, and just as he pulled it out he looked in the direction of the door and said "Come in, come in," and Carla slipped in beside me.

"Where have you been?" I whispered.

"I'll tell you later."

Just then Andrew walked over to where we were sitting, and my heart sank. Friends don't talk through friends' card shows. I was sure he was going to ask us to leave. He looked down at Carla.

"This young lady," Andrew said to the crowd. (Note: Our class has twenty-two students in it, all of whom, except Ellen Essoff, who thinks she is too mature for birthday parties with magic shows, were sitting at Andrew's feet.) "This young lady," he repeated, "just got here." Carla blushed and sank low, which is a hard thing to do when you're sitting on the floor.

"What is your name, please?"

"Carla," Carla said softly. Her face was bright red.

"Carla, ladies and gentlemen, was not here when I shuffled the cards. She was not here when I cut the deck. Therefore I am going to ask her to come up here and help me with this trick. It's called—sorry, Pinky—The Jacks' Party."

Carla stood up and I had to resist the urge to say, "Hey, I actually asked to be Andrew's assistant," and pull her back down, but she moved quickly to take her place next to Andrew.

"Okay," Andrew said, "I want to tell you a story.

"The jacks were having a party," he began, and dealt the four jacks, face side up, into four separate piles, "and the first guests to arrive were the kings." Then Andrew dealt out the four kings, putting each king on top of one of the jacks. "Unlike this party, however, the jacks' party was very, very dull"—he paused—"until the queens arrived, bringing their dancing shoes and a lot of loud music." He put the four queens on top of the four kings.

"Oh no!" Andrew exclaimed, looking genuinely worried. "The neighbors must have called the police!" He dealt out the four aces, placing one on top of each pile. "And the police took them to jail for disturbing the peace." Andrew picked up the first pile and put it on top of the next pile and that pile on top of the next, until there was a single pile with sixteen cards in it.

"Oh my," Andrew said gravely, "I'm afraid there was an accident along the way and the police cars ran into each other." He handed the deck to Carla. "Would you cut this stack in half, please." Carla cut the deck and pushed it back toward Andrew. "Again," Andrew said. "And again. And again. And yes, just for good measure, again."

After she had cut the deck five times, Andrew said, "Thank you, Carla," and took back the cards and dealt the first four of them facedown into four separate piles, the next four on top of those, and so on, till there were four piles of cards, each with four cards in it.

"Phew!" Andrew said, pulling a red handkerchief from his back pocket and wiping his brow. "Phew!" he said again, stuffing it back where it came from. "Even though the party-goers had been separated during the accident, and even though they all got knocked about in the accident and"—he looked out over the audience with a look of concern on his face—"even though one of the jacks may have gotten a concussion, I'm relieved to report that by the time they arrived at the police station"—Andrew nodded to Carla, who turned over the piles, one by one, and held them up for us to see— "they were all together again!"

It was true: the jacks were with the jacks, the queens were with the queens, the kings were with the kings, and the aces were with the aces. Everyone clapped like mad and Andrew bowed from the waist. Then he waved a hand in Carla's direction, said, "Please thank my able assistant," and so we clapped some more and finally she sat down.

Andrew called Pinky up next, though not by name and not as "the birthday boy," but instead as "the guest of honor." He had Pinky cut the deck a few times, shuffle a few times, and then cut the deck some more.

"All right, Pinky," Andrew said seriously, riffling the cards, "tell me when to stop." Pinky let a few more cards go by and then pointed. "Stop," he said.

Andrew turned all the cards above that point faceup and

put them back on the deck, then spread the deck from the top till he reached the first facedown card. He put this card down on the table. He pulled out the next facedown card and did the same thing, and the next, and the one after that.

"This trick, ladies and gentlemen," said Andrew, "is called The Amazing Ace-Stopper, and I think you'll see why"—and at that very moment he flipped those four cards over, and every single one of them was an ace. The crowd clapped wildly. Pinky, who had been standing off to the side, stepped forward and high-fived Andrew. Andrew smiled, but only a little. He was wearing his game face.

There were a bunch more card tricks after that: something called Any Way You Count Them, and one called Get Money, and others I don't remember because I wasn't taking notes. (Note to myself: Try to remember to keep notebook and pen in back pocket. On second thought, maybe pencil, not pen. My jeans already have ink stains from where I sat on a pen.)

Then the show was over, and Mrs. Summers herded us into the dining room for cake before I could say goodbye to Andrew. We sang the birthday song, and Pinky blew out the candles and cut the first piece of cake—which went to Andrew, it turned out, who was just about to walk out the front door when Pinky's mom cornered him and made Pinky hand over the slice, which, being Pinky's, was neither too small nor too big.

"You were great," I told Andrew, who was in mid-bite.

"Thanks," he said. "It was fun."

Just then a couple of kids from the class (Joey Damatto, Chris Latham, and Justin Moorehouse) came up and asked Andrew to show them how he did Get Money. Andrew said that he couldn't give away trade secrets, though he could recommend a good book, and as I backed away I stepped right on Carla's foot and she screamed. All conversation stopped for a second, so everyone could hear me say "Sorry," and then it resumed, and I realized that I was really mad at Carla. I mean really mad.

"It was . . . *interesting* . . . that you got to be Andrew's assistant," I said.

"Interesting?" Carla said doubtfully. "I just got to the party early and he asked me if I'd help him and I said yes and he said, 'Okay, I need you to hide until it's time for the show to start, and then I want you to come in late,' so I went upstairs and played with Pinky's fish and waited till I heard Mrs. Summers say it was time for the show."

"How do you *play* with fish?" I demanded.

"Play, watch—it's the same thing," she said. And then, as an afterthought: "Why are you so mad at me?"

"Me?" I said innocently. "What makes you think I'm mad?"

"You," Carla said angrily. "You. Sasha Abramowitz. You might as well be carrying a sign."

"Well, excuse me," I said.

"What is it?" Carla insisted.

I knew it was small. I knew it was petty. And all I could say was "Andrew Hardy is *my* babysitter!" putting the emphasis on the possessive. ("Possessive": a vocabulary word and a word in grammar. Or, as my dad would say, a "twofer." "Twofer," which probably won't be on anyone's vocabulary list soon, means "two for one"—a twofer.)

"Andrew Hardy is your babysitter," Carla repeated dully. "What does that have to do with anything?"

"I don't know," I said miserably. The bridge of my nose began to burn. That's where my tears always start. "You got to be the assistant."

"Because I was here early," Carla insisted. "Janice had to drop me off on her way to meet my dad at the airport."

I nodded. I had forgotten that Cliff was away. Doing something with leatherback turtles in the Virgin Islands, I remembered.

"But anyway, why do you care?" Carla said, taking my plate out of my hands and putting it on top of hers and walking the whole thing over to the trash barrel, into which she stared for a moment. "You know, if we wash all these plastic spoons and knives and stuff we could send them to people who don't have utensils."

"Like in Kuala Lumpur?" we heard a voice ask. A deep, male voice. We both turned. It was Andrew. "Would you young ladies like to walk home with me?" he asked. We said we would. The party was breaking up, anyway—Pinky never opened his presents in public—and parents were arriving and having the last slivers of ice cream cake and talking to Pinky's

87

mom, so it seemed like a good time to leave. We said goodbye and thank you (Note to parents: I put this in especially for you) and walked out the door together, me and Andrew and Carla. Though I hadn't answered her, Carla's question was still on my mind. Why did I care that Andrew had asked her, not me, to be his assistant? I mulled this over a minute while Andrew unchained his bike. Then I came to this conclusion: I didn't know *why* I cared, I only knew that I *did* care.

14

(No, you're not going crazy, there is no Chapter 13 for the same reason most tall buildings don't have a thirteenth floor. Does anyone complain about that?)

Andrew, Carla, and I walked along Pinky Summers's street, Pine Marten Way, till we got to the intersection with Howard Avenue, me on one side of Andrew and his bike, Carla on the other. At Howard, Andrew and I said goodbye to Carla, who had to go to her second piano lesson of the week (Carla has a theory that playing the piano a lot will make her fingers grow), and continued on together, just the two of us. The few people who passed by gave Andrew a funny look—he was, after all, wearing a black shirt and a white tie, black pants held up by black suspenders, a pair of red high-top sneakers and, of course, his frayed Krieger Cats cap. I, on the other hand, was the picture of normalcy, in purple corduroy overalls and a striped top, which is why I'm pretty sure it was Andrew they were looking at, not me, though I guess they could have been looking at me and wondering why I was walking down the street with him. Never mind. If you think about these things too much you could go nuts.

"Uh, Andrew," I began, "have you ever considered wearing a different costume when you do your show?" I asked as unrudely as I could.

Andrew shot me a worried look. "What's the matter with this one? It's classic. Magicians always wear black shirts and white ties."

"Always?" I asked, raising my voice in such a way as to indicate to Andrew that I was raising my eyebrows, which he couldn't see, because we were walking side by side. I was just on the verge of saying "Isn't *always* a stereotype?" But I didn't get a chance, because Andrew said, "Okay, commonly. Magicians commonly wear black."

I stopped and looked at him a little smugly. "My point exactly," I said.

Andrew, who had stopped rolling his bike, looked exasperated. "What, Sasha?" he said. "What point, *exactly?*"

"Just because all the other magicians wear black doesn't mean you have to, too. I mean, it's not a uniform, is it? Don't you think a magician in green or purple or even pink would stand out?"

"Pink?" Andrew said. He started rolling his bike again.

"You think I should wear pink? Remind me to consult with you the next time I want to look like an Easter egg."

"You don't have to be so mad," I said, walking quickly to keep up with him.

"I'm not *so* mad," he said, smiling slyly. "I'm only so-so mad."

"Very funny," I said, but to tell the truth, I was relieved. I hate it when people are angry at me.

"So I was thinking," Andrew said, changing the subject, "how about when I come over to babysit weekend after next we work on a Drew Hardy mystery." I could tell from his tone of voice we had achieved a truce, though secretly I was still a little upset that he had asked Carla to help him out, not me. But have you ever noticed that sometimes when people do things that hurt your feelings and you tell them what they've done, they have no clue they hurt your feelings because whatever it was they did to you was of no consequence to them? (Note to readers: "Consequence" is such a popular concept in Mrs. B.'s class that she didn't even bother to make it an official vocabulary word. "There will be a consequence if you forget your homework," she likes to say. Or "There will be a consequence if you don't clean out your cubby." Or "The consequence for not learning this week's vocabulary list will be to have fifteen extra words next week.")

"Why so quiet?" Andrew asked. "We don't have to do it if you don't want to. I just thought it would be interesting and fun."

We were close to the campus now. I could just make out the Krieger chapel, and the science building where my mother works. "I didn't know you were going to babysit then," I said. "It's news to me. Which night?"

"Both. Your parents said they had to go away for the weekend with Danny."

"The whole weekend? Nice of them to tell me." I could feel myself getting upset again. Why was I always kept in the dark? First the thing with Carla this morning, now this.

"They just called last night and left a message. I haven't called them back. Maybe they were waiting to tell you till they knew."

"Knew what?"

"Knew what the deal was. Whether it would be me or Ellie Anderson or—"

"Oh!" I said abruptly, suddenly remembering the annual Trannell Academy retreat, when Trannell teachers and Trannell parents and their Trannell kids spend the weekend at a camp in New Hampshire working together in the garden, having three-legged races, and sitting around the campfire making s'mores. On the last day they pass around a Native American "Talking Stick," and anyone who wants to can say something about their feelings about the weekend. The Eraser would love it.

We had reached the Krieger campus, and any minute now Andrew would hop on his bike and turn left, and I'd head straight up the hill, past the kids lying on blankets on the grass as if it were a beach—studying, snoozing, listening to music, and making out. (Yes, making out. Don't blame *me*. I'm only telling you what I saw.)

But Andrew didn't get on his bike, and I didn't head up the hill. Instead we just continued to stand there talking.

"Look, Sasha," Andrew said, "I'll tell your parents no, if you don't want me to do it."

"No!" I said sharply, and loudly enough to cause the two girls nearest to us to sit up and stare at us and scowl. "I mean, yes," I said. "I do want you to." The girls lay back down, in unison, and started to read again. "It'll be good. Great. Better than with Ellie Anderson last year."

"Oh?" Andrew said. It was obvious that he wanted to chew on his cap, but it was locked in under his bike helmet, so all he could do was touch it, which he was doing a lot.

"As soon as Mom and Daddy left last year she called up her ridiculous boyfriend—you probably know him, his name is Lloyd—"

"Lloyd Walker?"

"I don't know. Lloyd. He's tall and sings 'One Hundred Bottles of Beer on the Wall' when you're in the shower so you don't stay in too long. He says anything past eighty-three is a big fat waste of water."

"He runs recycling on campus," Andrew said.

"I know," I groaned. "I had a cold when he was over, and

when he saw that I was using tissues to blow my nose, he pulled out a bandanna from his pocket and told me to use it instead because it could be washed."

"And did you?" Andrew asked.

"What do you think?"

Just then the bells in the steeple of the Krieger chapel rang out a single note, which caused Andrew to look at his watch and jump on his bike. "Shoot," he said. "I'm almost late. We have a game this afternoon." He started to pedal away. "Two weeks," he called over his shoulder. "Think of a mystery we can work on. It will be fun. And I promise I won't ask you to blow your nose into a piece of cloth."

15

"What do you think of red?" Carla asked the next Tuesday, out of the blue (okay, I know it's a pretty poor joke, what can I say?). It was five minutes past eight in the morning and we were in the Early Resources Room, which makes it sound like the resources themselves have gotten to school before the bell instead of us. But there we were, hanging out, waiting for the regular day to begin, Carla working on a maze and me doing a hidden word search, looking at that very moment for the word "bracelet," which turned up running diagonally from the left-hand corner, because our parents all had to go to their monthly departmental breakfasts.

"What do you mean, 'red'?" I asked.

"You know, red. The color. Red," she repeated, as if I were an idiot.

"I know what red is, obviously," I said. "But what *about*

red? Red lipstick—I think it's creepy. Red turtlenecks—okay, unless you have red hair, since it could clash. Red hair? Very cool. Red lollipops—yum, my favorite. Red Life Savers—too cherry—"

"Okay, okay, okay." Carla held up her hands. "Stop!" she said.

I stopped.

Carla took a deep breath, sighed, and paused cautiously, as if she was waiting to see if I was going to start up again. "Okay," she said when she was convinced I wasn't. "Pinky and I were thinking of starting up a business and calling it Red," she said quickly, looking at me out of the corners of her eyes. (Note: If you are wondering how she did this, try looking at your left shoulder without turning your head and you'll see what I mean.)

"Pinky and you?" I said. "Pinky? You and—"

"Yes, Pinky," she said, pretending to be a little bored by my obvious surprise. "You know, the boy you met the second you moved to Krieger. The one whose party we just went to."

I nodded. What I had really meant, and what I did not say, because it was just too hard, was "Why him?" Meaning, "Why not me, Sasha M. C. Abramowitz, your complete and utter and obviously *ex*–best friend?" First the thing with Andrew. Now this. Maybe we weren't such good friends after all. Maybe that was just an illusion. An article I once read in *New Moon* said you should expect a certain number of your friends to "move on" as you all got older. Was that what was happening? Was Carla "moving on," while I stood still?

"What about your trash for the Kuala Lumpur project?" I asked weakly, pretending to look for the word "aluminum" in the word search so I wouldn't have to face Carla. (Note to the Eraser: Yes, you guessed it, I had tears in my eyes.)

"Oh, I can still do that sometime," Carla said cheerfully. Just then the bell rang. I crumpled up the word search and tossed it in the garbage can, picked up my knapsack, and walked out of the Early Resources Room with Carla right behind me.

"Pinky got this book for his birthday and he asked me if I wanted to do it with him," Carla said, rushing to keep up.

"What book?" I said over my shoulder. "Do what with him?"

"Start a business," she said, catching up. "It's called *Biz Kidz*. The book he got for his birthday. From me, actually." She laughed a tiny little nervous laugh.

We had reached our lockers, which were side by side, and were both busy with our combinations. "But you already have a business," I said. "With me." My locker popped open and as the door swung outward I was confronted with my own face passing by in the little mirror that a previous locker-user had glued to the inside door. There was no denying it. My eyes were red around the rims from the effort of holding back my tears.

"Is there anything wrong, Sasha?" Mrs. Blank said as I walked into room 6B. "Your eyes are so—"

"Red," I said loudly so Carla, who was right behind me, could hear. "I must be allergic to *something*."

"I'm sorry to hear that," Mrs. Blank said. "There are tissues on my desk if you need them. I just put out a new box."

It turned out that Mrs. B. had just put out a new box because she had gone through the old box herself that morning. "Crying tears of joy," she told us. We looked at each other. What was she talking about? (Note: Have you ever noticed how teachers always seem to know the details of your life and how you hardly ever know the details of their lives? Mrs. B. had been my teacher for seven months and all I knew about her was that her first name was Christine, that she was married to Mr. Blank—first name unknown—and that both Blanks were graduates of Krieger College.)

"Okay, listen up, people," Mrs. Blank said, clapping her hands together. Usually when she clapped her hands and said "Listen up, people," she looked kind of stern, but not today. Today she had a big smile on her face. She was beaming at us (through her hooded eyes). We got quiet in a hurry. You could have heard a pen drop—and then we did, when someone in the back row accidentally knocked one off his desk. Mrs. Blank took a deep breath and let it out slowly.

"I've been trying to think of the best way to tell you this," she began, and stopped. Apparently she hadn't figured it out yet.

"Okay," she said, taking another deep breath, "I'm not sure exactly when, but sometime in the next few weeks I'll be going on maternity leave."

Like everyone else in that room, I looked at Mrs. B. Specifically, and also like everyone else, I looked at her stomach. I knew this was rude, but what could we do? Mrs. Blank is not a big woman. She was wearing a peach-colored blouse and a pair of whitish pants. There was no sign that a baby was growing under there. None.

We all must have been confused because instead of smiling back at our teacher or asking questions, we sat there dumbly. Not dumbly as in "stupid," but dumbly as in not moving or saying anything.

Just then Mrs. Blank turned, took a folder off her desk, and pulled out a photograph that she held up to the class.

"Here she is," she said proudly. The picture showed a small baby girl in diapers and a yellow shirt sitting in a playpen. She had skin the color of toast (when you use the "light" setting) and dark curly hair.

"George and I," Mrs. Blank said. "Mr. Blank and I," she corrected herself—(so his name was George)—"will be going to Guatemala to pick her up as soon as we get the word."

"What word?" Carla asked, forgetting to raise her hand.

"You didn't raise your hand," Mrs. Blank told her.

"Sorry," Carla said and put her hand up. "What word?" she asked again.

Mrs. B., who can be a stickler for classroom rules, was probably just about to tell Carla that, though she had raised her hand, she, Mrs. B., had not yet called on her—but then she didn't. Instead, she just pretended she had called on Carla, which let her answer the question. "The letter from the orphanage saying Lindy is ready. That's what we're calling her: Lindy Clemens Blank. Clemens was my name before I married Mr. Blank."

Though I knew I was supposed to be thinking about that little baby, all I could really think about was my father and how, under no circumstances, should he find out that that kid's middle name was going to be Clemens because he'd be knocking at the Blanks' door that night, standing on their front porch explaining why they should consider adding "Samuel" to their baby's name, as in Lindy Samuel Clemens Blank, because you couldn't get more American than Mark Twain, and Mark Twain was Samuel Clemens and Samuel Clemens was Mark Twain, and, either way, Professor Barney Abramowitz could be very persuasive.

Mrs. Blank pointed to the world map that was taped to the wall. "Anyone care to tell me where Guatemala is?" she asked.

Pinky Summers raised his hand. "Near Mexico?" he asked.

Mrs. Blank nodded. "Very good, Pinky," she said. She pointed to a green speck on the map. "Here," she said.

"And what do we know about Guatemala?" she asked

brightly. Not "what do *you* know?" but "what do *we* know," as if we—our whole class—were the same person. Which, I'm happy to report, we are not.

Mrs. Blank went to the board and wrote the word "exports" at the top and underlined it once. "I want you to write this word down," she said, turning to face the class again. "You never know when it might appear on a vocabulary test. Does anyone know what it means?"

Patty Gundersen raised her hand. "I think it means like when there are slaves and you make them do your work and you don't pay them and you're really mean to them and—"

Mrs. Blank made the time-out sign with her hand. "Actually, Patty, I think you're thinking of the word 'exploit.' Maybe we'll have that word some other time. Anyone else want to tell me about 'export'?"

Pinky raised his hand, then waited for Mrs. Blank to call on him (unlike some people we both know). "It's the stuff one country sells to another country. Like cars."

Patty Gundersen laughed. "Who has ever heard of a Guatemalan car," she said dismissively.

"No," Pinky said patiently. "Like Japan. You know, Hondas and Toyotas. We have a Honda Civic."

"Hondas are now made in Ohio and Toyotas in Kentucky," a boy in the back called out (without raising his hand, I may add). It was Ryan Hodges, who only opens his mouth (1) during lunch, and (2) when the conversation is about transportation.

Mrs. B. clapped her hands. "Okay, people. People, okay,"

she said. "Pinky is right. An export is a product or a service sold by people in one country to people in other countries. Any idea what Guatemala might export to this country?"

Carla waved her hand frantically. "Snakes!" she said loudly when Mrs. Blank called on her.

"Snakes?"

"Yeah," Carla said. "I'm pretty sure my father brought back a rare poisonous snake from one of his field trips to the Andes."

"The Andes are not in Guatemala," Mrs. Blank said. "Anyone else?"

"Sorry," Carla said quietly. I knew she was embarrassed—Carla hates to be wrong in class—and secretly I was glad.

"Anyone?" Mrs. Blank repeated, scanning the room with her eyes.

The class was silent. And then, softly, so it was hardly audible, someone said, "Babies," and someone else—me—laughed out loud.

"Sasha!" Mrs. Blank said sharply.

I could feel my face begin to burn with shame. "But I didn't say anything," I protested. (Note: Technically this was true. I didn't *say* a word. Didn't that count for something?)

"No, you didn't," Mrs. B. agreed, and I felt better, but only for a second. "You didn't have to, Sasha," she said, just as the recess bell rang.

"I'm sorry," I managed to mumble to Mrs. Blank, who stood by the door as we filed out.

Mrs. B. nodded. "I expect more from you, Sasha," she said.

Recess was no fun, what with Carla huddled with Pinky, talking, I guess, about Red, and neither was the rest of the day. Mrs. B. didn't bring up Guatemala or babies or her maternity leave again. At home my father said, "Why so glum, puddle?" which is an inside joke for anyone who has read the Narnia books and remembers the character Puddleglum. When I told him, he put on one of those philosophical "these things happen" faces, which is supposed to be comforting but never is because just because these things happen does not mean that when they happen to happen to you they don't count. When these things happen to you they actually count more because, obviously, it's you to whom they are happening.

"Why don't you write Mrs. Blank an apology," my mother suggested after a dinner I barely touched.

"That's a great idea," Daddy said, retying his bow tie. Usually he takes his school clothes off after school, but tonight he had a meeting.

"What would I say? 'Dear Mrs. Blank, I'm sorry I laughed today in class when someone said that Guatemala exports babies'? Isn't that pretty stupid? Won't it make her feel worse?"

My father ignored this. "How about 'I'm sorry I hurt your feelings. I look forward to meeting your baby.' "

"No kid would write that," I said.

"Then put it in your own words," he said, and so I did. "Dear Mrs. Blank," I wrote,

I am really sorry I laughed in class today when you were talking about your baby. I can't wait to meet her. Maybe we could have a contest in school to give her a nickname.
Sincerely yours, Sasha Abramowitz
P.S. I really am sorry.
P.P.S. I'll bet you and Mr. Blank are really excited and can't wait to go to Guatemala.
P.P.P.S. I think it's really cool that you told us about it.

Though Mom offered me a stamp, my plan was to drop the note on Mrs. Blank's desk first thing in the morning so she'd get it faster. Good plan, impossible execution. (Note: No, I don't mean someone got killed or, in this case, didn't get killed. I mean that I couldn't do what I set out to do.) When I got to school, a man with reddish hair and a bushy reddish beard and bifocals that rested on unusually long ears was sitting at her desk. A substitute.

"Oh," I said, startled to find him there. "Is Mrs. Blank gone? To Guatemala? Already?" I asked. The man eyed me suspiciously through both levels of his glasses, as if I were guilty of a crime I hadn't yet committed.

"They don't tell me anything," the man said grumpily, "except where to find the lesson plan, except that I can't even find that."

This I took as a good sign—and a bad one. Good, because Mrs. B. would never go on maternity leave without leaving the most detailed lesson plan in the universe, including every single vocabulary word she expected us to know by the time Lindy Clemens Blank was our age. Bad, because, obviously, it was my fault. I had run that woman right out of school. I had made her disappear just like that. (Warning: If you actually say something like this out loud, certain people—meaning, specifically, adults—will accuse you of believing that you have magical powers. On the other hand, I would just like to point out that if my father turns on the radio to listen to the Red Sox and the Red Sox are winning and then the other team hits a grand slam and ties it all up, Daddy will immediately turn off the radio because he secretly believes that it was his fault the other team scored and that if he hadn't turned on the radio the Red Sox would still be ahead. *So what is that?*)

I rushed out of room 6B and walked quickly to the principal's office, where I just about ran straight into the principal, Mr. Baer, who is as big as—yes, you guessed it—a bear (grizzly, not black). (Note: Mrs. Blank once told us that the way to remember the difference between the word "principal," as in "the person in charge of your school," and "principle," as in "a rule or a law," is that the principal who runs your school ends in "pal." Get it? The principal is your *pal*, though this is not true for Mr. Baer, who has a puffy pink face that makes him look like he's just about to explode.)

"Where do you think you're going, Miss Abramowitz?" Mr. Baer boomed at me.

"Mrs. Blank—" I started.

"Mrs. Blank is not here today," Mr. Baer said. His large body—specifically, his large stomach—was blocking the entrance to the office.

"I know," I said. "I just need to get this letter to her before, you know, she leaves for Guatemala, and I thought one of the secretaries would have her address."

"She'll be back tomorrow," he said. "Give it to me. I'll put it in her box." He stuck out his hand the way people (i.e., adults) do when they want you to spit out your gum. I handed it over reluctantly, worried for an instant that he would open it himself and read it out loud, over the P.A. system. But then I had another thought: he had said that Mrs. B. would be back tomorrow. *Mrs. B. would be back tomorrow!* I did my best to stay cool and not show Mr. Baer that he had just spilled the beans—or, in this case, the bean: Mrs. B. would be back tomorrow. I had not run her out of school after all.

It turned out that Mrs. Blank liked my idea about the nickname contest and that she wasn't mad at me at all. (Apparently, Mr. Blank had to have a bunion removed from his left foot *and* had car trouble, so Mrs. B. just decided on the spur of the moment to drive him around, which is why Mr. Grump had been sitting at her desk the day before.) She said we could leave our nickname suggestions in a manila envelope she would tack to the corner of the bulletin board nearest the door.

"Will this be a simple majority, a two-thirds majority, or a four-fifths majority?" Pinky Summers asked. (His father is chairman of the political science department at Krieger College, if you couldn't tell.)

"None of the above," Mrs. Blank said. "George and I—Mr. Blank and I—will take your suggestions with us on the plane, and if one of them seems to fit, we'll choose it. You've got a little less than two weeks, people, because," she said, pausing to pull something out of her handbag, "we got this yesterday." She waved an official-looking piece of paper through the air. Then she walked from desk to desk so we could all get a better look at it. There was a gold seal at the top, and all the words were in Spanish, but you didn't have to be able to read it to know what it was: Lindy Clemens Blank's permission slip to come to the United States.

16

On Thursday, when I got home, there had been a phone call from Andrew Hardy. Daddy had taken the message, which meant that he must have come home for lunch after spending the morning at the barbershop. Underneath the "Sasha, call Andrew Hardy" note was another one: "K. Cats game this afternoon. If you want to go, call me (at the office) at 3:30." I looked at the clock on the wall. It was just after three. I considered calling Andrew back first, but realized that he'd already be at the field, warming up. I took my homework out of my knapsack. It was a research "drill," where we had fifteen minutes to answer five questions using more than one reference book. "Question 1: Name two countries that border Guatemala. Question 2: What is the largest city in Guatemala? Question 3: List at least two natural resources found in Guatemala." I stopped reading; I could see where this was going. Luckily my parents had recently bought a set of encyclopedias from a kid at the college who was selling them to raise money to pay his tuition (or maybe it was for a new car), and we also had a *World Almanac*, so I had the answers in no time. (Did you know that people in Guatemala blow glass and grow bananas? Well, now you do.) Just as I was finishing up, the phone rang. It was Daddy.

"Hey, kiddo, are we on for this afternoon?" No "Hi, honey," or "How was your day?" just "Are we on?" And then, before I could answer he said, "Sasha, I think today is the day." Anyone else hearing this would probably wonder "the day for what?" but I knew. Daddy says this practically every time the Krieger Cats play ball. What he meant was that today was the day the Cats were going to break their seven-year losing streak and win a game. You'd think the odds were in their favor. You'd think it was like when you flip a coin—even if it just keeps coming up tails, it's got to go the other way eventually.

"When should I meet you?" I asked.

"How's the homework?"

"Very, um, Guatemalan," I said.

"Good, good," Daddy said absentmindedly. "Meet me in fifteen minutes on the library steps. We'll walk over together. Maybe we'll catch batting practice."

Only my father, Barney Abramowitz, would be excited to see a team that has lost something like twenty-six games this season alone take batting practice. But that's my dad. "The Greeks could not have written a better drama than this," he likes to say, but if you ask me, where's the drama when one team—ours—never wins? I thought drama was when you didn't know how things were going to end up, but Daddy says, "No, Sasha, that's suspense. Drama goes much deeper than that. Drama plumbs the soul." (Note: Homonyms, ugh. "Plumb," like what a plumber does, versus "plum," which you eat; "sole," the bottom part of your foot or your shoe, versus "soul," definitely not part of your foot. If I were inventing a language, Rule #2, after "It should be in English," would be "No words that sound the same and have completely different meanings.")

I called Carla. Cliff answered and said she wasn't home yet. "The Cats are playing this afternoon," I told him. "I'm going with my dad if Carla wants to meet us there." He promised to give her the message if she got home in time.

"Could you tell her I called, anyway," I said. I didn't want her to think I was sore anymore about Pinky Summers and Red. If she was "moving on," I wanted to keep up with her.

Daddy was on the library steps talking to Frank Benjamin, who was scratching Tripod between the ears. She must have followed Frank from the dining hall because she was licking the roof of her mouth over and over again as if she had peanut butter stuck there, which she probably did.

They both said hi to me, and then Frank asked Daddy if he should take the dog to the dorm so she wouldn't follow us to the game.

"Thank you," Daddy said. "Professor Abramowitz will be home soon, so you can tie her up in the garden.

"The dog, not my wife," Daddy added, laughing. "Come on, Sasha."

It was a ten-minute walk to the playing fields, and as we went I informed my father that Guatemala exported sugar, bananas, coffee, blue shrimp, white shrimp, brown shrimp, and watermelon. I told him about Guatemalan textiles and blown glass. "Did you know that Guatemala has the biggest economy in Central America?" I asked him.

Daddy, who I expected to laugh, or at least smile, gave me one of his knowing I-am-a-college-professor-and-therefore-full-of-wisdom looks. "I know you think it is ridiculous, Sasha, but just wait. Someday, like when you are writing your first book, some of those facts about Guatemala might come in handy. You never know."

"I will never remember those facts," I said, exasperated. He just didn't get it. "Ever," I said for emphasis.

"Talk to your mother," Daddy said. "I think you'll be surprised."

But you know what surprised me—and Daddy, too? When we got to the ball field the other team was on the field, shagging flies and tossing balls and stretching. Our team, though, the mighty Krieger Cats, was gathered in the dugout, bats aside, mitts off, watching Andrew Hardy do a card trick. "This one is called Eight Threatening Kings," I heard him say.

111

17

"Why are they doing that?" I asked Daddy.

"It's not like warming up has actually helped them before," a voice behind us said. I knew this voice. It belonged to Carla.

"Hey," I said.

"Hey," she said.

"Where's Pinky?" I asked, trying to sound like I cared and didn't care at the same time.

"Dentist," Carla said. "He forgot, and his mom forgot, and then the dentist called to see where they were and he had to go."

"Oh," I said. (Note to readers: Have you ever noticed how sometimes people tell you more than you really want to know?)

"Hmm," my father hummed. "Hmm. Hmm." He sounded like an engine that couldn't quite get started. Daddy was staring at Andrew and the other Krieger Cats—Andrew was now doing a trick called What's on Your Mind—and so were the members of the other team. One by one they lowered their bats and dropped their gloves and watched from a distance as Andrew pulled cards from the deck and showed them around.

"What's he doing?" they asked each other, and added, "That's really weird, freaky," and then their coach, who had been looking, too, clapped his hands and said, "Okay, okay, knock it off, boys. Back to work. You don't have anything to worry about."

"Oh, I get it," Daddy said, more to himself than to us. "It's all about focus. He's trying to get their attention."

"Like hypnosis?" Carla asked. "Like he's hypnotizing them?"

"Sort of," Daddy said, reaching into his pocket and pulling out a pack of Jolly Ranchers. Both Carla and I automatically stuck out our hands so he would give us each one, which he did.

"Let's go ask Andrew if that's what he's doing," I said to Carla. I was feeling good now. No one had to say it, but I was pretty sure that we were back to being best friends.

"No!" Daddy shouted, and grabbed my arm. "Don't go!" And then, more calmly, "Don't interrupt him. You never know. You just never know."

The fact was, though, what you never knew with the Krieger Cats was how badly they were going to lose. Would it be by seven runs or nine runs or, as it was once, by seventeen? Andrew was playing shortstop. A boy named Raja Williams was pitching. His catcher was Doug Jacoby. Silliman "Silly" Andresen was at first.

Carla and I finished our Jolly Ranchers—I think she chewed hers, actually—and stuck out our hands for another. "Please, sir, may we have . . . more," Carla said in her best Oliver accent to get Daddy's attention.

"What? Oh. Yes. I mean no," Daddy said. "Not until the Cats get their first run."

We both groaned. In unison.

(Note to the Eraser: I thought behavior modification was when a person gets a reward for doing something that some-one like you wants them to do, like when Danny gets his baseball cards *after* he says hello and how are you and all the rest. But in this case it wasn't like Carla and I could "earn" a Jolly Rancher by getting a run since [1] we weren't on the team; [2] we couldn't be on the team; and [3] we would never, ever, be in scoring position, if you see what I mean.)

You might think, given the Cats' habit of losing, that the games would not be tense—but if you did, you'd be wrong. And when the Cats took the field after a thirty-minute warm-up that included exactly no balls being hit and precisely the same number being tossed and caught, the tension was so thick you needed a band saw to cut it. Raja, our pitcher, was taking the mound cold.

"Ball one!" the umpire called as Raja's first toss veered off to the left and the catcher almost had to crawl to get it. A groan went up from our side of the bleachers, though Daddy, I noticed, had not made a sound. Instead, he was twirling and untwirling his bow tie around his finger the same way he did when he said he had a poem "coming on," as if it were a head cold or a migraine.

"Ball two!" the umpire called as the ball landed loudly in the catcher's mitt. This one was high and inside.

"Joker's wild!" Andrew yelled to no one in particular when the ball was back in Raja's hand and Raja was getting ready for his windup.

"Strike one!" the umpire called as the ball rocketed over the plate.

Daddy, who had been looking pretty grim, allowed the corners of his mouth to lift up a tiny bit, maybe two degrees at the most. If you didn't know him as well as I do, you'd probably think he was grimacing. (Note: When Mrs. B. gave us "grimace" as a vocabulary word last fall, she said it was one of those words that we'd probably find ourselves using more than we ever thought we would. At the time we all . . . grimaced . . . but she may have been right after all.)

Raja's next pitch was even faster than the one before it, but this time the batter got a piece of it with his bat, probably just by luck, and the ball sailed high into the air but back, be-hind home plate, and the catcher, Doug Jacoby, stood up, flipped off his mask, held out his mitt, and let the ball drop in like a hole in one.

"Out!" the umpire yelled as our side cheered and clapped and whistled. Anyone walking by would have thought the Cats had scored a run, not gotten an out.

"That was special, wasn't it, girls?" Daddy said after the other side went down one, two, three, and Andrew stepped up to the plate for the Cats. I concentrated all my attention on Andrew, trying to send him a telepathic message: "Get a hit." But he didn't. Not one. And neither did batters two and three. Our side was back in the field before Andrew had had a chance to do a three-sixty with his cap, with a quick stop halfway around to chew the bill.

I am going to spare you the details of the next seven in-nings, for which you should get down on your knees and thank me, because exactly nothing happened. Not one run was scored. Not one Jolly Rancher was handed over to me or Carla, and to tell you the truth, neither of us noticed. Because although it was true that our team did not score a single run, which under normal circumstances would mean that we were losing, neither did the other team. So far, going into the ninth inning, Raja Williams had pitched a perfect game. My father was beside himself. (Note to self: I don't get this. How can someone be in one place and, at the same time, be standing next to himself?)

"This could be it, girls," Daddy said, hardly above a whisper, as if he'd jinx it if he talked louder.

It was the top of the ninth. Raja was still on the mound. Everyone—meaning everyone in the bleachers and everyone on the field except for the catcher—was standing. Some Krieger girls started chanting "RA-JA, RA-JA!" but they were shushed by the distinguished professor of baseball poetry, my father, Barney Abramowitz. "Give him room. Let him breathe," Daddy said, as if Raja had passed out and were being crowded by curious onlookers.

If this were a Disney movie, Raja would now go on to strike out the next three batters, one, two, three. But that is not how it happened. He did strike out the first batter. He did strike out the second. The score was still 0–0 and would stay that way if he could strike out the third. Then Krieger could come back at the bottom of the inning, get a run, and win. I'll bet every single person in the Krieger bleachers was thinking the same thing. Everyone, that is, except for Carla, who grabbed my left hand, turned it palm down, and looked at my watch. "I wonder if Pinky is out of the dentist's yet," she said.

"Ball!" the home plate umpire called. Everyone around us booed. Raja, who thought it was a strike, who couldn't believe it wasn't a strike, went back to the pitcher's mound and managed, in less than two minutes, to get to a full count: three balls, two strikes. Whatever happened next would probably decide the game.

Doug Jacoby came out of his catcher's crouch to talk to Raja. He put his arm on Raja's shoulder and said something that caused the pitcher to shake his head no. Then Doug smiled and slapped Raja on the butt with his mitt. As he was trotting back to his place, we all heard Andrew say, "Our ace is not wild." Then Raja, looking almost giddy, went into his windup.

The pitch went whizzing over the center of home plate. It was perfect. Everyone could see that, even the batter, whose bat collided with the ball in a very loud way. He dropped the bat and ran like mad for first base, kicking up a cloud of dirt behind him, but it was too late. He was already out. His line drive had been caught by Andrew, who was being mobbed by his teammates.

"This could really be it," Daddy whispered to himself. "Really." His jacket was off and his bow tie was hanging loose around his neck and he was sitting on the edge of the bleachers with his eyes closed and his hands on his knees. He looked like he was praying. I decided that I should pray, too.

"Dear God," I began. I know it sounded like I was writing God a business letter, but I thought it would be rude if I just started in with "Please let Krieger win," without some kind of salutation. ("Salutation" was a vocabulary word when we did our letter-writing unit. A salutation is the greeting at the beginning of a letter. I can't remember what the "sincerely yours truly love" thing at the end is called, though.) "Dear God," I started again, "I really hope you are here today, which I kind of doubt, since there are wars and people dying and famine and lots of other horrible stuff going on in the world, so why would you be here, at Krieger, watching a stupid baseball game, unless you are like Daddy and just love baseball, which brings me to another thing: Daddy says that baseball is the national sport of the United States, so does that mean you are an American?"

"Oh no," Daddy groaned, which basically stopped me in mid-prayer, before I got to the part where I asked God to help the Cats win.

I looked down at the field. Our pitcher, Raja Williams, was at bat. That was bad news. Raja is the weakest hitter on the team. Another way of putting that is: Raja Williams had pretty much struck out every time he was at bat for three years. He was pathetic. Even he said so.[3]

Raja squared his shoulders and bent his knees. He took a couple of practice swings. Then he stepped up to the plate just in time to slide his right hand up to the top of the bat and bunt. The ball dribbled off the wood and Raja took off, running so fast I almost couldn't see him. I couldn't believe

---

3. See the *Krieger Campus Clarion* (vol. 47, no. 26, p. 7) interview with Raja where he says, "It's pathetic, what a lousy batter I am. I guess it goes to show that you don't have to be good at everything to play a game you love."

it. Could God be answering my prayer, right then and there? Even though I hadn't finished it, it probably didn't matter, since God would have known what I was going to ask even before I did. In any case, the ball was "hit," the opposing pitcher was scrambling to get it, and Raja Williams, for the first time in his Krieger career, was sitting pretty on first base, looking as awestruck as everyone else.

Andrew was up next. This was exciting. In case I didn't say this before, Andrew is the very best hitter on the Krieger Cats. Daddy says that if Andrew played for a better team he'd be a star, which doesn't make complete sense since you'd think he'd be more of a star on a crummy team, where he'd stand out. ("Yes, Sasha," Daddy tried to explain one time, "it's true that Andrew is the brightest light on the Cats, but what does it matter when he is eclipsed, time and time again, by the poor playing of his teammates?" When I said I still didn't get it, Daddy turned off all the lights in my bedroom except the one on my desk. "The light is Andrew," Daddy said. Then he took a big book and held it up. "The book is the team." Then he put the book in front of the light and it blocked almost all of the light so there was just an aura around the edges of the book. "I rest my case," Daddy said, returning the book to the bookshelf and turning on the other lights.)

The crowd, which had grown since we first got to the game, was cheering and yelling and making a big racket, but Andrew stood there like he heard nothing. He had a vague smile on his face and he held the bat high off his shoulder, waiting.

The catcher made a sign with his fingers. The pitcher shook his head. The catcher made a different sign. The pitcher shook his head. Now the pitcher looked angry. He stepped off the mound, spit, stepped back on, narrowed his eyes, and threw.

"*Oh my God!*" Carla shrieked, right in my ear, at the exact same moment as Andrew fell to the ground with blood pouring out of his mouth and nose. His whole head was a fountain of blood. (Note to readers: I am sorry if you think that is disgusting. It *was* disgusting. But that's what happened.) He had been hit in the face with the ball. For a moment nobody moved. Then, it seemed, everyone was in motion—the coach, the trainer, the umpire, and a couple of Krieger Cats who ran onto the field and were surrounding the pitcher.

"Is he going to be okay?" I asked Daddy.

"I hope so," Daddy said. This was bad—he was being noncommittal.

"Is he in a coma?" Carla said. "Is he going to die?"

"Andrew Hardy is not going to die," I said angrily. It seemed mean of her even to think it. Disloyal.

"Oh, I wish Pinky was here!" Carla wailed.

"Pinky?" I said in disbelief. Now I was really mad. Furious, in fact. "Pinky Summers? What for?"

"He'd know what to do," Carla said quietly.

"What to do?" I said. "Pinky Summers would know what to do? Pinky Summers is an eleven-year-old boy. Even the coaches don't know what to do." And they didn't. One wanted to put Andrew on a stretcher. Another one was afraid to move him. It was a big mess.

"Twelve," Carla corrected me. "Pinky Summers is twelve."

Just then Andrew sat up, looked around, lifted his hand, and made a little wave. His cheek was already swollen and a fresh river of blood ran down his face. He said something to the coaches and then he lay back and let them lift him onto a stretcher and carry him off the field. I pretty much forgot how mad I was at Carla (again) and focused on Andrew.

"Where are they taking him?" I asked out loud, to no one in particular.

"To the infirmary," Carla said. "Don't you think so, Professor Abramowitz?"

"It's more likely that they'll take him directly to the hospital," Daddy said. "Poor Andrew. I really thought they had a chance." I could see tears gathering in his eyes, though I guess, technically, you can't say he was crying because none of them spilled over the rims.

"This is too tragic," Daddy said, "even for me."

18

The good news: For the first time in seven years, the Krieger Cats did not lose.

The bad news: For the 328th time in seven years, the Krieger Cats did not win.

The better-than-bad-but-not-as-good-as-good news: The game was suspended.

The extremely bad news: Andrew Hardy had to spend the night in the Krieger Community Hospital, "for observation."

"They make it sound like Andrew is some kind of science experiment," I said to my mother, who was making chicken à la Abramowitz[4] for dinner. "Under observation."

---

4. The recipe goes something like this: Take a chicken and put it in a pan with carrots, red potatoes, garlic, olives, leeks, green beans, zucchini, asparagus, and whatever else is in the crisper that is not lettuce or lettuce-like. Sprinkle the whole mess with parsley, thyme, and olive oil,

"They are just being careful," she said, throwing a couple of parsnips into the pan. (Have you ever had a parsnip? Probably not. I only ate one the first time because I was little and thought it was a really pale carrot. Now I'm used to them.) "Any injury is dangerous when it is near the brain," said Mom. This was not just her opinion, she explained, but a medical fact. It had to do with possible interruptions in the flow of oxygen and blood to the brain and how that affects the neurons, synapses, and dendrites, and within half a minute she had lapsed into one of her lectures. Sometimes my parents can be such professors. It's like they can't help themselves.

"Andrew lost a lot of blood," I said, interrupting her.

"Did he, Barney?" Mom said, sliding the chicken à la Abramowitz into the oven.

"I just said he did," I said. "Don't you believe me?"

"Of course I believe you, dear," she said. "I was just wondering what your father thought."

"But why?" I insisted.

"Sasha!" my mother and father said at the same time, though Daddy didn't have a clue what this discussion was about. He had been studying the box scores in the newspaper, which showed the Red Sox three games behind the Yankees, and was just reacting to the eye-rolling sound of my voice.

------

put it, uncovered, in the oven, and cook till it's done. If you want to know what temperature to cook it at, and for how long, you are going to have to get in touch with my mom, Professor Marcia Abramowitz, care of Krieger College.

The phone started to ring and I picked it up. It was Daddy's friend Neil Levine. *Dr.* Neil Levine. "Yes. We do know him. He's Sasha's . . . Right away," Daddy said, and hung up. And then he said to us, "Get your things, we have to go to the hospital." Because he didn't say which things, we all walked out of the house empty-handed.

"Wait a minute," I said, when we were more than halfway to the car (which has to be parked in a special faculty lot on the other side of campus), and ran back to our apartment and grabbed a pack of cards. I met my mother running toward me, as I ran back toward my parents. "I forgot to turn off the oven," she called, trotting past.

It was about twenty minutes after Dr. Levine called when we all finally piled into my father's (disgusting) blue Honda, which was closer than my mother's (tidy) blue Honda, and started out for the hospital.

It occurred to me that no one had said what, exactly, was wrong with Andrew. It occurred to me that *no one* had said he *wasn't* dying. (Note: This year, Mrs. Blank explained all about double negatives. Personally, I think it is very cool to be able to use words like "no" and "not" to mean "yes.") It occurred to me that no one had said why Dr. Levine had called us, either. It occurred to me that my head was filled with all sorts of thoughts, most of them scary and sad, and that my heart was racing and my palms were clammy.

"What's going on with Andrew?" I managed to say. I knew if I asked if Andrew was dying they were going to say no, even if he was. It has been my experience that parents are like that: they like to protect kids, even if the kid doesn't want or need to be protected.

"He needs a blood transfusion," Daddy said.

"Turns out you were right about how much blood he lost," Mom said.

Ordinarily I would have taken some satisfaction in being right and in Professor Abramowitz being wrong (though, technically, she hadn't been wrong, she had only been—*Alert! Vocabulary word coming up*—skeptical), but in this case I was completely sorry to have been right.

"What's a blood transfusion?" I asked.

"It's when a person needs more blood and gets it from donors," Mom said.

"I don't get it. What are donors?"

"People who donate their blood."

"That's weird," I said. "Don't they need their blood?"

"Most people can afford to lose about a pint of blood without their body minding," she said. "You've seen those signs around town for blood drives, haven't you?" I guessed that I had, but I also guessed that I hadn't paid any attention to them.

"The thing about giving someone blood, Sasha," Daddy said, "is that their blood and your blood have to be the same type. Otherwise it could cause complications. Type O is the most common. That's what most people have."

"Is that what Andrew has?"

"No, he has some other kind. That's why the doctor called. Neil wants to see if our blood matches Andrew's. It probably doesn't, but it's worth a try."

"But what if it doesn't?" I asked. I was completely scared now. Completely. Andrew was going to die. Andrew Hardy was going to die. A completely selfish thought came into my head: Now he wasn't going to be able to babysit when my parents went on the Trannell retreat, which made me feel even worse. One, for thinking it. Two, because it was true.

The entire Krieger Cats baseball team was filing out of the hospital as we walked in. There was Raja Williams and Doug Jacoby and the second baseman, whose name I can never remember, and none of them was smiling and all of them looked grim. On the other hand, all of them looked surprisingly clean-shaven. But that wasn't the only odd thing about them: all of them had what sort of looked like stitches, drawn with marker under their left eyes. "In solidarity with Andrew," the one whose name I can never remember told us as he passed by.

"Casper!" I said out loud when we were in the elevator. "Casper Wylie," I said.

"What is it, Sasha?" my mother said, and though she sounded a little angry, I knew her well enough to know that she wasn't angry, just worried.

"Nothing," I said. The second baseman was named Casper Wylie. Everyone called him "the Ghost."

19

Andrew was lying in bed wearing a blue hospital gown and his chewed-up Krieger Cats baseball cap (of course), watching the ball game on an overhead TV. (Note: When I say "the" ball game, I mean "the" Red Sox. When I say "a" ball game, I mean a baseball game between any two teams, neither of which is the Red Sox.)

"What inning?" Daddy asked.

"Bottom of the fourth," Andrew said. His voice sounded funny—faraway, and like there were marbles in his mouth. "The stitches make it hard for me to talk," he said, reading my mind.

"I brought you a pack of cards," I said, taking them out of my pocket and putting them on the table next to Andrew's bed.

"Thanks, Sasha," he said, but made no move to pick them

up. That's when I noticed how pale his skin was, and the big purple bruise on his cheek. It was the size and shape of a baseball. You could even kind of see where the ball's seams had been.

"Hello, Abramowitzes," a voice said. Dr. Neil Levine came striding into Andrew's room and stopped. "What inning?" he asked, looking up at the TV.

"Fourth," we all said. He nodded. "Score?"

"The Red Sox are up by two," Andrew said. "Sasha brought some cards," he told the doctor. "If you want to see that trick." It turned out that Andrew had recently done one of his magic shows at Blair Levine's seventh birthday party. Blair Levine is Dr. Levine's completely annoying daughter—but let's not go into that.

"Maybe later," Dr. Levine said. "Right now we've got work to do. How are you, Marcia?" he said to Mom, who was sitting in the chair next to Andrew's bed, studying his chart.

"Fine," she said, looking up at him over the top of her reading glasses. It was then that I saw the tall metal pole behind Andrew's bed with the bag of blood hanging from it, and the tube that went from the bag into a needle taped to his arm. To tell the truth I don't know how I missed it, except that the Eraser says that sometimes we see only what we can see. When he first said it (about two years ago, when I asked him why, if Mom and Dad are so smart, it took them so long to realize Danny had "problems"), I thought it was completely dumb. I mean, come on, of course we can only see what we can see, right? But just then it was sort of like with Casper Wylie, the Ghost, in the elevator: it dawned on me that sometimes people block out what's hard for them to deal with. My parents probably had not wanted to see that Danny wasn't normal, just like I hadn't wanted to see the bag of blood and the needle just below the crook of Andrew's elbow. (Note to myself: Find out the connection between "crook," as in elbow, and "crook," as in thief.)

"I guess you can see what we're up against," Dr. Levine said, walking over to Mom's side of the hospital bed. If Andrew heard this, he gave no sign. Both he and Daddy were completely absorbed by the game. But I heard.

"You mean the B negative blood," Mom said.

"That's just part of it. The easiest part, really. Ideally, we'd like to get the blood from sources we know. It's just safer that way." He paused, took a look at the TV screen, and smiled. Manny Ramirez had just cracked a double, bringing two runs in. "Even more ideally, we'd like to have the immediate family. Increases the chances for a perfect match."

Mom looked confused. (Mom rarely looks confused.) "*Perfect* match?" she said.

"Bone marrow," Dr. Levine said, and they both nodded and looked serious.

"Have you called the parents?" Mom asked.

"Not exactly," Andrew said, turning to face her. Apparently (unlike Daddy), he *had* been listening all along.

"Andrew is adopted," Dr. Levine said in a very matter-of-fact way.

"Oh," Mom said. "I see."

Here is something interesting (at least to me) that I've noticed about Professor Marcia Abramowitz. She is always taking things people tell her and turning them into problems to be solved. It's like the whole world is an equation or a science project. So when she said "I see," what she really meant was "I don't see yet, but I will, and so will you, because I will show you." Or something like that.

"Do you know anything about Andrew's birth parents?" Mom asked Dr. Levine, who shook his head no.

"We've got a call in to Andrew's family in Arizona, and also one in to their doctor, which might help."

"Don't hold your breath," Andrew said quietly.

"Why?" Mom asked. "They won't call back? Why won't they call back?" She sounded indignant.

"They'll call back," Andrew said, almost whispering, "but they won't be helpful."

"They won't be helpful? Why won't they be helpful?" Mom said even more indignantly.

"Don't you think I haven't asked about my birth parents?" Andrew said. "They always find a way to let me know they don't want to talk about it. I told myself that when I turned eighteen I'd try to find them on my own, but then I didn't."

"Why not?" I asked. We were all, even Daddy, looking at

Andrew lying in the bed, his eyes sputtering like a candle about to go out.

"I am very tired now," he said, and then without warning, he was asleep. Mom took off his baseball cap, which had slipped over his eyes, and put it on the pillow next to him like a stuffed animal.

"What is going on, Neil?" Daddy asked after Dr. Levine had herded us out of Andrew's room, into the hall. "He got hit with a baseball. Kids get hit with baseballs every day. "Why the blood?"

"Oh, that reminds me," Dr. Levine said. "Do either of you know your blood type?"

"I'm A positive," Mom said.

"Barney?"

"O positive."

"You sure?"

"Certain."

I would like to say that this is when Dr. Levine turned to me and said, "Well, Sasha, you are Andrew's only hope right now," whereupon I was whisked away to the blood bank by a handsome (male) nurse to have my blood drawn and analyzed while my mother said, "But, Neil, her age. She's so young," and Dr. Levine said, "I know it's a risk, Marcia, but it's one I think even her mother will agree we have to take," and then the handsome (male) nurse said, "Wow, you're only eleven?" and "You're a really cool kid," and "I'd never have been as brave as you are when I was your age," and then a really tall (female) nurse jabbed a long needle attached to a glass tube into my arm and the tube began to fill with a thick red liquid—*my* thick red liquid—and the very tall (female) nurse said, "Now, that didn't hurt too much, did it, Sasha?" to which I gave no reply because I wanted her and the handsome (male) nurse to see exactly how brave I was, and then the tall (female) nurse did some things with my blood that included shaking the test tube, adding something that looked like blue dye, and putting a couple of drops on a slide, which she slid under a microscope. "Would you look at that," the tall (female) nurse said to the handsome (male) nurse. They both said, "Ooooh" and "Ahhh." Then they both turned to me and stuck out their hands for me to shake. "Sasha Abramowitz," the tall (female) nurse said, "you alone will be able to save the life of Andrew Hardy." "Congratulations," said the handsome (male) nurse, pumping my arm.

But this did not happen. Dr. Levine asked my parents their blood types and didn't even bother to ask me mine. My blood didn't count. My blood was too young. I didn't count. My friend Andrew Hardy was lying in a bed, in a hospital, dying, probably, and I wasn't going to be able to help him. (Note to the Eraser: Here is how I felt: terrible.)

"Well," Dr. Levine said, "I think we should bank your

blood, anyway. We may need it for something else." He didn't say what that was, and no one asked. Instead, my mother said, "Explain the blood loss, Neil."

"There was a clotting problem, obviously," the doctor said, "but we don't know why. We ruled out the obvious—"

"Like hemophilia," my father broke in.

"What's hemophilia?" I then broke in.

"We'll tell you later," Daddy said.

"It's when your blood is missing the part that lets it clot and form scabs, so you just keep bleeding," Dr. Levine said, turning to me.

"Scabs are disgusting," I said.

"Sasha!" both my parents said at once.

"They may be disgusting, Sasha," Dr. Levine said, "but they are necessary. Without them, people could bleed to death the first time they got a cut or even a nick. Most of us wouldn't make it out of diapers."

"So it's not hemophilia," Mom said. "What else?" She looked determined, like she wanted to figure this thing out right now, standing in that hallway, and like she wasn't going to leave, or let Dr. Levine go, until she did. But his beeper was ringing, and he had to go.

"I'll walk you to the elevator," he said. As we went, he reeled off the names of some other diseases he was sure, or pretty sure, Andrew did not have.

"What about leukemia?" Mom asked.

(Note: When I was little, I thought leukemia was an actual

person, a man named Lew Keemia, because Daddy had a cousin who had it and one day, when Daddy was talking to someone on the phone, I heard him say, "Cousin Mark had leukemia," and I pulled on his pant leg to get his attention and said, very urgently, "When?" "When, what?" Daddy asked, putting his hand over the receiver so the person on the other end wouldn't hear us. "When did cousin Mark have Lew Keemia over for supper?" I asked. Daddy smiled and held up his finger and mouthed the words "Wait a minute, I'll tell you when I'm off the phone," which he did. That's how I found out that Lew Keemia wasn't a person—though I bet if you searched all the phone books in the world you'd find a Lew or Lou or Lewis Keemia or Keemeeyah somewhere—it was some kind of blood disease—but not, Dr. Levine was saying, the kind Andrew Hardy had.)

"That is why," Dr. Levine concluded, "it would be really good to get ahold of Andrew's birth parents, or at least the mother. We'd have more to go on. Right now we're in the dark, which is not a good place to be with a bleeder."

We had reached the elevator. "The blood bank is on three," Dr. Levine said, pushing the DOWN arrow. He gave Mom a quick hug and squeezed Daddy on the shoulder. Me he didn't touch. Not with his hand or any other part of his body. "Your friend is in good hands," he said, looking at me directly. "Try not to worry."

Before I could say anything, or even think of anything to say, he turned and walked back the way we had just come,

135

pausing for a moment at the nurses' station before continuing down the hall, past the room where my friend Andrew Hardy lay sleeping, with someone else's blood racing around his veins. I could hear the elevator coming; it was maybe two seconds from opening when I had what may have been the most amazing, most important, most stupendous (Note: Mrs. Blank put that last word on the vocabulary list, she said, so we would not grow up thinking that the word "stupendous" had anything to do with the word "stupid"—as a man she once overheard in the supermarket did), most brilliant (please don't think I'm bragging), most awesome, most miraculous thought of my entire life up until then.

"Marie Curie!" I said—well, shouted—which caused every single person waiting for an elevator (there were three of them), all the nurses at the nurses' station and the doctors standing there, too, and every patient and family member and friend in the hall to stop and look in my direction, which meant, too, in the direction of my parents, who hissed my name in unison, which meant "What are you doing, shouting like that, and in a hospital; have you lost your mind? And by the way, please stop embarrassing us." But before they had a chance to say this, I took off down the hall in the direction of Dr. Levine's back as it disappeared around the corner, almost tripping over a cart filled with dinner trays and a man walking with crutches. And then I turned the corner, too, expecting to see Dr. Levine strolling on ahead, but he wasn't there. He was absent. It was like space aliens had come and taken him away. Dr. Levine was completely and utterly gone.

I stood there a minute catching my breath, trying to figure out what to do next. I think I'm like my mother that way: she'd already be thinking up Plans B, C, and D. And speaking of my mother, there she was, running toward me, with Daddy right behind.

"Dr. Levine!" I called, because at that very second I also saw him coming out of a room to my left. MEN the sign on the door said.

Dr. Levine turned, saw me standing there calling him, saw my parents racing down the hall, and looked completely confused. "Sasha? Is something wrong?" he asked, walking over.

"I think I may know what's wrong with Andrew," I said quickly.

It was at this very moment that my parents reached us, and neither of them looked too pleased.

"You don't just run off like that," Daddy said, panting.

"That's right," Mom said. "I'm sorry if Sasha is bothering you," she said to Dr. Levine.

"Not at all," the doctor said. "Sasha here believes she may know what's wrong with Andrew Hardy." Then he winked at my parents, meaning "Ha, ha, ha, what a ridiculous idea, but ha, ha, ha, let's let her tell us." Ordinarily, under normal circumstances, this would have made me furious, but these were not ordinary circumstances, so I decided to ignore it. "So what is it?" he said to me.

All the adults were looking at me. Suddenly I felt very small, and very silly, and very quiet.

"Sasha," Daddy said.

I gulped, took a deep breath, and exhaled. "I think Andrew has the same thing Marie Curie had," I said. I looked at Dr. Levine, thinking that he would be nodding and smiling and on the verge of apologizing to me for winking at my parents. And he *was* smiling, but in an amused, superior way, and my heart sank.

"What disease was that?" Dr. Levine asked.

"Plastic anemone," I said.

Dr. Levine's smile broadened. "Last time I checked, an anemone was a little sea creature," he said. "I don't know about plastic ones, though."

"Sasha," Daddy said, "Dr. Levine is a very busy man."

"Sorry," I said quietly, and turned to go.

"Thanks, Neil," Mom said apologetically. She put her hand on my shoulder, pushing me along. She didn't have to push hard. No one wanted to be gone from that man and that place more quickly than I did. Me, Sasha Abramowitz, moron and loser.

But then I felt another hand on my shoulder, this one holding me back.

"Wait a minute, Sasha." It was Dr. Levine. "Did you say Marie Curie had it?"

I nodded. "And Eleanor Roosevelt."

Dr. Levine stopped smiling. His expression turned serious.

Dr. Levine gave me a funny look—he kind of scrunched up his nose and pursed his lips. (Note to myself: Find out the connection between "purse" as in pocketbook and "purse" as in what you do to your mouth.)

"Really, Neil, it's all right," Daddy said.

Dr. Levine waved him off. "It's okay, Barney," he said. "This is very interesting to me. I think Sasha may be on to something. I think what she meant to say was aplastic anemia."

"That's what I did say," I insisted.

"Sasha!" my mother said sharply.

Dr. Levine didn't seem to hear. "Aplastic anemia can cause clotting problems. And it often comes on spontaneously, for no apparent reason. The bone marrow just begins to produce too few blood cells."

"Marie Curie got it because she was exposed to so much radiation," I said.

"Yes, that's another cause," the doctor said, "though probably not the cause of Andrew's problem. In young people there is often no cause. Or, at least, no cause that we can find."

"How is it treated?" Mom asked.

"That's the good news," Dr. Levine said. "Pretty much the way we're treating Andrew's condition now. Transfusions. Antibiotics. Other meds. Bone marrow transplant if nothing else works and if we find a donor." He looked at his watch. "I'm late for a meeting in the ER," he said, taking a step away from us. "The other good news is that people don't die from it the

139

way they did in Marie Curie's day. Or in Eleanor Roosevelt's, for that matter."

"That is good news," Daddy said, sighing.

Dr. Levine looked in my direction. "Thanks, Sasha. That was very good thinking." Then Dr. Levine turned to go one way and the Abramowitzes turned to go the other. Daddy looped his arm through mine on the left and Mom looped her arm through mine on the right, and there we were, a living wall of Abramowitzes, moving down the hall of the Krieger Community Hospital at nine forty-five at night.

"Oh my gosh!" I groaned five steps later, and stopped. "I'll be right back," I said to my parents, breaking out of their grip. Luckily, Dr. Levine hadn't made it far down the hall because he had stopped to tie his shoelace. (Note: Because of my own "issues" with shoelaces, due to the trouble I've always had with fine motor skills, I have never been much of a fan of shoelaces. You would think this would have encouraged my parents to buy me sneakers with Velcro, to make my young life easier, but think again. Professor Barney Abramowitz and Professor Marcia Abramowitz do not believe in making life easier. Also, they thought that if I had Velcro sneakers I'd never learn to tie my shoes. Which, at long last, I did. So it was for the very first time in my eleven years on the planet, as I moved quickly toward Dr. Levine that I said to myself, "Thank goodness for untied shoelaces.")

"I just had another thought," I said, leaning over the doctor's back.

"What's that?" he said, not looking up.

"When I did my report on Madame Curie." I stopped.

"Yes?"

"Which I did this year, for my sixth-grade report.[5] Well, even though Andrew wasn't exposed to radiation like Marie Curie, couldn't there be a different reason he got sick?"

"Well, yes, Sasha, of course," he said, standing up. "Some people get aplastic anemia because they have certain other diseases, or because they take certain medications or because they've been exposed to certain bacteria or fungi."

"Okay," I said. I had heard enough. "But you can't tell Andrew I told you."

Dr. Levine looked at me in a strange way. "I can't tell him you told me what?"

"Andrew chews his cap. His Krieger Cats baseball cap. He wears it, plays in it, chews it, puts it down in the dugout, on tables and chairs, everywhere. Including his mouth. All the time."

"I see your point," Dr. Levine said.

"Promise that you won't tell him it was me. He loves that cap."

"Don't worry," the doctor said. "It will be our secret." He stuck out his hand and we shook on it. "You know, Sasha, if you keep this up, you should really consider becoming a doctor when you grow up."

---

5. If you want to read my report on Marie Curie, see Appendix 2.

I felt a blush coming on. I looked down at my feet, where it seemed to have started. "I want to be a writer," I said. "And maybe a pastry chef."

"Well," Dr. Levine said, "those are both noble professions, too." Still, I could tell he didn't mean it. What Dr. Levine meant was that he really believed that his job was the best job in the world. The most noble. Which got me to thinking. Was being a writer noble? Was being a pastry chef?

In the car, driving home, Daddy said that if you are lucky in life, the work that is best for you to do will call to you like a friend in a crowded room and you will just go in the direction of that voice.

"You keep on listening, Sasha," he said when we were saying good night. "I know you'll hear it."

20

The next day was school—more on Guatemala—so I couldn't get over to the hospital until afternoon. I went home after school, played with Tripod, ate a toasted bagel with peanut butter, did my homework (*even more* on Guatemala), and finally, around three forty-five, rode over to Krieger Community. Andrew was still in the same room, and blood was still dripping into his veins, but he was awake and his skin no longer looked gray. A new blue and red and unchewed Red Sox cap sat high on his head.

"What do you think?" Andrew said, taking it off and showing it to me.

"I like it," I said.

"Me too. Only I'm not supposed to chew it. Doc thinks that's what might have made me sick. Some bacteria or fungus." He then proceeded to repeat to me everything I had said to Dr. Levine, and I proceeded to listen as if I had never heard it before.

Just as he was finishing, there was a knock at the door and both Andrew and I looked up to see Carla and Pinky standing there holding a huge bag of peanut M&M's. Peanut M&M's are just about Andrew Hardy's favorite "food." Why hadn't I thought to bring some?

"Thanks, guys," Andrew said. "That's really nice of you. If you want, you can put them over there." He pointed to the windowsill, where, it seemed, every member of the Krieger Cats had already put a big yellow bag of peanut M&M's, which made me feel like even more of a jerk. I was probably the only person to visit Andrew Hardy in the last twelve hours who did not bring him a bag of peanut M&M's. I gave Carla a completely dirty look, which she returned by looking surprised. "What?" she said out loud.

"Nothing," I said.

"You don't own him, Sasha, even if he was your babysitter first," Carla said under her breath. I looked to see if Andrew had heard, but he hadn't. He was shuffling a deck of cards—my deck of cards, to be precise—so he and Pinky could do a card trick called All the King's Horses. This reminded me of something I had wanted to ask Andrew the day before.

"What was all that stuff in the dugout yesterday, instead of warming up?"

"Oh, that!" Andrew laughed. "We were just trying to psych out the other team. And also to concentrate. Card tricks are really good for concentration. They quiet the mind. Most of winning and losing is about focus. It's almost all mental."

"You mean that if the team went to see Dr. Serkowsky, they would have a better chance of winning?" Carla asked, looking directly at me. Dr. Serkowsky, Dr. Edgar Raymond Serkowsky, for anyone who has lost their focus, is the Eraser, and this was about the meanest thing Carla Smith had ever done to me—not that anyone else in the room knew it. But she knew. She knew how much I hated going to the Eraser and how embarrassing it was that I had to go. She knew it all because she was—or, rather, *had been*—my best friend.

"It couldn't hurt," Andrew said. "A number of professional athletes and sports teams hire sports psychologists to help them visualize being winners. There's this Olympic skater who spent hours every day listening to tapes of his psychologist telling him he wasn't going to fall during his gold-medal free-skating routine, and then he won the gold medal. I was sort of thinking along the same lines, and when I told the coach he said, 'Yeah, Hardy, go for it. It can't hurt.' So I figured what the heck, and came up with a thirty-minute routine. It almost worked, too."

Andrew stopped talking and sank back onto his pillow. He handed the deck of cards to Pinky. "I'm getting real tired, guys," he said.

"We'd better go," I said to Carla and Pinky. Andrew waved at us weakly. "Thanks for stopping by," he said, and shut his eyes.

The three of us left the room and ran straight into Dr. Levine, who was coming down the hall with a very large man who had dark circles under his eyes and eyebrow hairs that looked long enough to braid. He was wearing a white lab coat, just like Dr. Levine's, and he had a stethoscope looped around his neck and an ID card attached to his lapel that said "RUFUS STACKPOLE, M.D."

"Oh, Sasha," Dr. Levine said warmly when he saw me. "There's someone I'd like you to meet. This is Dr. Stackpole. He runs our hematology department. Do you know what hematology is?"

I looked at them blankly. "Oh, I do," Carla volunteered. That's one of the things my father teaches at the college. Snakes."

The men smiled. "That's herpetology," Pinky whispered.

"Oh," said Carla, coloring. So she was embarrassed. Did I care? Yes, yes I did. I was glad.

"Dr. Stackpole runs our blood program," Dr. Levine said. "Hematology is the study of blood. Rufus, this is the young woman I was telling you about, Sasha *Marie Curie* Abramowitz, who diagnosed our ballplayer, Andrew Hardy."

Dr. Stackpole stuck out his hand and squeezed mine. "Very impressive work, Sasha," he said. "And how old did Dr. Levine say you were?"

"I'm eleven," I said.

"Let's see," he said, "if you're eleven now and you graduate from college in ten more years, then have four years of medical school, that's fourteen. Okay, fourteen years from now, you come and see me and you've got yourself a job.

"Seriously, Sasha, I sometimes hire smart kids like you to work in my lab in the summer. When you turn sixteen, if you're interested, you come see me."

"Don't hold your breath, Rufus," Dr. Levine said. "Sasha here wants to be a writer."

"And a detective," Carla piped up.

"I do not," I hissed at her. "You do. Did."

"Being a doctor *is* being a detective," Dr. Stackpole said. "That's what makes it interesting. As far as being a writer, there's no reason you can't do both. You're probably too young, but have you ever heard of William Carlos Williams?"

As a matter of fact, I had. Daddy has a copy of one of his poems hanging in his office at the college. "He was a poet, I think," I said.

Rufus Stackpole and his braidable eyebrow hairs looked at me like I was some kind of genius. "And a doctor," he said. "Do not forget it. William Carlos Williams was a doctor *and* a writer."

"That girl is astonishing!" we all—me, Carla, Pinky— heard Dr. Stackpole say to Dr. Levine as they walked into Andrew's room. My heart, and all the blood in it, swelled till it was too big for my chest. I was . . . astonishing!

"So how is Red?" I asked Carla and Pinky when we were in the elevator.

"It never really got off the ground," Pinky admitted.

"But it's only been a few days," I said.

"I think that sometimes you just know when something is not going to work out," Carla said. She looked at me intently. It seemed to me that she may have been talking about our friendship even more than she was talking about their business failure, but I let it go. Pinky, as usual, was his clueless, good-natured self. If you had to have a boyfriend, you could do a lot worse than choosing Pinky Summers.

It was right then and there, basking in the glow of Dr. Stackpole's praise, that I decided to declare a truce once and for all. If Carla wanted to hang out with Pinky Summers, fine. If Pinky Summers wanted to hang out with Carla, fine. But they were my friends, too, especially Carla, and like it or leave it, they were going to have to hang out with me, too. I mean, even married people have friends, don't they? It was at this very moment that I had what I hoped would turn out to be the second most important, most stupendous, most awesome idea of my life. Andrew had said he wanted Drew Hardy and Associates to go back into business, and why not? Why not have Drew Hardy (aka Carla Smith) and her associates (Sasha Abramowitz *and* Pinky Summers) try to find Andrew Hardy's birth mother?

21

"You know, kids, finding someone who does not want to be found and whom other people would not like found, can be almost impossible," Mrs. Summers said to us the next day. We had picked Pinky's house to meet at because Mrs. Summers made the best cookies and because, out of our eight parents, we decided she was the one most likely to be encouraging. And now she was saying that finding Andrew's mother was "almost impossible," which was at least not saying that it was completely and totally impossible.

"The very first thing you'll need," she went on, "is Andrew's permission. This is a very serious and emotional thing for him. You can't just try to find his mother without letting him know that you're trying, and you can't try to find his mother if he objects. Understand?" Mrs. Summers made each of us, in turn, say that we understood. "Now, take this plate of raspberry thumbprint cookies over to the hospital and see what Andrew has to say."

What Andrew had to say was—nothing. He wasn't in his bed. A nurse walking by said she thought he was downstairs in the cafeteria. The three of us looked at each other in surprise. Andrew was not only out of bed but dressed and eating in the cafeteria? Andrew, who the day before had been hooked up to an I.V. with blood running into his arm? What was going on? Here was another genuine mystery for Drew Hardy and Associates to solve.

22

The Krieger Community Hospital cafeteria was a noisy and humid place that smelled like coffee and mashed potatoes. It was filled with sleepy-looking doctors and worried-looking people who were probably not doctors. (Clue: They were wearing street clothes and did not have stethoscopes hanging from their necks.) It took a while to find Andrew; I almost didn't recognize him without his baseball cap on. He was sitting with two grownups, a man and a woman. The man was wearing a plaid shirt over a T-shirt and looked annoyed. The woman was in a plain cotton dress. She was small and Asian.

"They can only be two people," I whispered to Carla and Pinky.

"Of course they are only two people," Carla whispered back.

"No," I said, "I mean that they can only be Andrew's parents. I wonder when they got here."

Andrew's mother must have seen us pointing, because she reached across the table and touched Andrew on the arm and said something that made him turn around. The bruise on his cheek had turned yellow under the purple and looked like a flower painted with watercolors, pretty in a way, if it hadn't been in the middle of his face. Andrew waved us over and introduced us, but when that was done the three of us just stood there not knowing what to do, while the three of them just sat there not knowing what to do. Then Pinky suddenly remembered the cookies and pulled them out of his knapsack. Andrew's mother's eyes filled with tears, and she said she was happy that even so far from home Andrew had friends who were as kind as we were.

"You haven't tried the cookies yet," Carla said. It was a joke—like maybe the cookies were so bad they really weren't much of a gift—and Andrew smiled, which made his mom smile (shyly), which made Pinky smile, and then Carla, then me. It was like a game of telephone, but without words. Mr. Hardy just sat there looking stern. Finally, when the twenty-six muscles of my face that let me grin were completely worn out, I said, "Andrew, could we talk to you a minute," and he said, "Sure," and got up from the table. We had decided this on the way over—that I was going to be the one who asked, since Andrew was, after all, both Carla and Pinky agreed, *my* babysitter.

"What is it?" Andrew asked when we were out of earshot of his parents.

"Umm," I began. "Umm," I started again.

Andrew looked amused. "I can tell this is going to be good."

"You know how you wanted me to come up with a mystery for Drew Hardy and Associates to solve?" I paused and took a breath. "Well, I think I did. What if we—the three of us"—I motioned toward Carla and Pinky, who were standing awfully close to one another, I observed—"and you, if you want to, when you feel better—try to find your, try to find your, try to find—

"The woman who had you," I concluded.

"My birth mother?" Andrew said with surprise.

We wagged our heads enthusiastically. "Yeah," I said.

Andrew glanced in the direction of his parents.

"I don't know," Andrew said slowly. "I already have a family. Finding her doesn't matter." His voice trailed off. "No," he said more clearly after a while. "It's not a good idea. Not now."

"Not now!" I said, my voice (and anger) rising. "What about the bone marrow stuff? What about finding out if anyone you're related to has the same thing? This is serious, Andrew."

"I know it's serious, Sasha," Andrew said. "I know it better than anyone else. But Dr. Levine says I don't need any more transfusions, at least for now, and that the bone marrow thing is not necessary, and if worse comes to worst, he'll take out my spleen."

"Take out your spleen?" I said indignantly, even though I had no idea what a spleen was, or where it was, or why the doctor would take it out. "You're willing to have the doctor cut you open rather than finding the woman who had you?" I was on a roll. I was outraged. I was just about to say something really mean, something that would show Andrew Hardy exactly how I felt about his decision, that the reason he wouldn't do this was that he was scared, scared to find out the real truth, and that he was a chicken, when Pinky sneezed. It was one of those really big sneezes, and a lot of people turned around to see where it had come from, and my anger subsided enough to let Andrew squeeze me on the shoulder and say thanks but no thanks without me insulting him.

"Looks like Drew Hardy and Associates is out of business, again," I said to my friends when we were outside, wheeling our bikes across the parking lot.

23

Monday morning when I got to school, Mrs. Blank was moving around room 6B like an industrious ant, straightening a pile of books here, sharpening a box of pencils there.

"Listen up, people," she said as soon as the bell rang. "I've got an announcement to make." We all stopped talking and looked at our teacher. Had she (and George—I mean, Mr. Blank) decided on one of our nicknames already? Were they leaving for Guatemala right away? Were we going to spend the morning playing Guatemalan *Jeopardy!* again, like we had on Friday? ("Guatemalan Folk Songs for ten jelly beans," "Central American Wars for twenty jelly beans," "Guatemalan Cuisine for forty jelly beans.") Things in room 6B had never been more up in the air.

"In a few minutes," Mrs. Blank began, holding her hands

in front of her like she was praying, "Mr. Baer will be bringing in the teacher who will be taking my place while I'm on maternity leave. She'll be here all week learning how we do things in 6B. I want you to be courteous and helpful. No funny business." She stopped and stared at the row of boys in the back. "No funny business," she repeated. "Then, after I'm gone next week—"

"Next week?" a chorus of those boys said, without raising their hands.

"Yes," she said, unclasping and clasping her hands. "Isn't it wonderful? By this time next week, George and I—Mr. Blank and I—will be on the plane for Gwah-te-ma-la."

There was a knock at the door and Mr. Baer walked in trailed by a young woman with long blond hair pulled back into a high ponytail that was fastened by a silver barrette. She looked familiar to me, like I had seen her before. And then I knew.

"Class," Mr. Baer said, "Mrs. Blank has someone she wants you to meet."

"Oh yes!" Mrs. Blank said enthusiastically. "Can you say hello to your new teacher, Ms. Flum?"

"Hello, Ms. Flum!" we all shouted.

"Hello," Jenny Flum said back. "How are you this morning?"

We all answered, "Good." Then Jenny Flum said, "Good, I'm glad to hear it. It's good to be here."

"But what about Broadway?" I wanted to ask. "What about

the movies?" Hadn't Jenny Flum heard acting calling to her like a friend across a crowded room? What had happened?

And then it occurred to me. Then I knew. Danny. Danny had happened to her. The swimming pool incident had made a mess of her life. It had stolen her dreams. It had drowned the friend who had been calling to her from the other side of the room.

24

To get Jenny Flum in the swing of things, Mrs. Blank had her take attendance. She was supposed to read off our names, and if we were present we were supposed to say "Here." Pretty simple stuff. Since my last name starts with the first two letters of the alphabet, it's been first on the attendance list every year but second grade, when a boy named Tommy Aaron joined our class for the year his mother was teaching at Krieger College. There is just no way to beat out someone whose name begins with double "A's."

Mr. Baer left, and Mrs. Blank handed the attendance list to Jenny Flum, and Jenny Flum called out the first name: mine. I expected to see a flicker of recognition, but there was none.

So I was right. That day with Danny flipping and flopping in the pool, and me gone without a trace in Mrs. Mendelsohn's yellow Lincoln, and Daddy's car crashing into the tree had wrecked her life. She even seemed to have that disease where your mind erases all the bad things and leaves a big hole where people and places and things that happened used to be. I sank low in my seat, then sat up straight. If she didn't remember me, what did it matter? "Here!" I said, raising my hand.

I kept waiting all day for Jenny Flum to come up to me and say something to indicate that she remembered me, and remembered living in our house, our real house, the one with the pool in the backyard, but she didn't. Either Jenny Flum really did have that memory loss thing or she was still a really good actress. But then, when the afternoon bell rang and we were all heading out to our lockers, Jenny Flum said, "Sasha Abramowitz, would you please come see me a minute," which caused a couple of the boys to say "Uh-oh, Sasha, what did you do?" If only they knew.

"Sasha," she said, shutting the door, "I can't believe it's really you. You've grown up so much. How old are you now?"

"Eleven," I said.

"You've gotten so big," Jenny went on. She was like one of those relatives you see once a year who pinch you on the cheek and say, "Let me take a look at you," and tell you you've grown, as if you yourself may not have noticed it. Jenny wanted to know how my family was, which I guess meant Danny, too, so I told her we were all fine, that Mom was still teaching brain stuff and Daddy was still writing at the barbershop, and that we didn't live in the house with the pool anymore, we lived at the college, and that Danny went to a school called Trannell Academy in Massachusetts, but that he might be coming home for the summer. "But they always say that," I said, trying to reassure her that she and my brother would not be spending time in the same town anytime soon.

"What about Broadway and acting?" I asked her. "Or Hollywood and movies?"

Jenny smiled one of her many Jenny smiles, this one kind of sad-looking. "How about a half-empty dinner theater in East Cricket, Rhode Island? How about 'Marian, the Librarian' in Kalamazoo? I know that everyone has to start somewhere, but eventually my parents convinced me that the most prudent thing to do—do you know that word, 'prudent'? In this case it means 'practical' [Note: Clearly Jenny Flum liked vocabulary as much as Mrs. B.]—would be to get my teaching certificate so I'd have, quote, something to fall back on, in case the acting didn't work out. So here I am. Your teacher." She gave me a hug. I gave her a hug back.

When I told them at home that Jenny Flum was now my teacher, both Mom and Dad wanted to know when she could come to dinner—as if I might actually know the answer. But I asked her the next day, and she said she could come the day after that, and so it was all set that Jenny Flum would come to Aster West on Wednesday at 6:00 p.m. Meanwhile, Andrew was still in the hospital and his parents were still in town and basically camped out in his hospital room, so I didn't stay long when I went to visit. The Krieger Cats were doing surprisingly well—for the Krieger Cats. Since Andrew's "accident" they had lost another game, but only by two runs. Members of the team would be at the hospital sometimes when I got there, but more often than not it was just me and Andrew and his mom and dad, neither of whom said much. His dad flipped through out-of-date issues of *Reader's Digest* that he found in the waiting room, and his mom did needlepoint. Maybe they talked more when I wasn't there, but I kind of doubted it. Andrew's mom had a kind, gentle face, so it didn't really matter that she was so quiet. But his father—his father was different. His father scared me. His silence seemed angry. I bet he spanked his kids when they were little.

On Wednesday Jenny Flum came exactly at six, bringing a bouquet of flowers for the table. Daddy gave her a big hug, and Mom gave her a big hug, and then they all hugged me. Like it or not, Jenny Flum had played a big part in the life of the Abramowitz family. We weren't Broadway, and we weren't the movies, but life with us had certainly been dramatic. *Danny Abramowitz's Nuclear Meltdown*, starring Danny Abramowitz and Jenny Flum, costarring Sasha Abramowitz in the role of the runaway child.

We were just about to sit down to chicken à la Abramowitz—no, not the chicken à la Abramowitz Mom had made the week before, the night we had to go to the hospital, but this week's edition—when the phone rang. In some families there is a rule that you don't answer the phone during dinner, but in our family the rule is that you pick up the phone anytime, under any circumstances, because it might be a Krieger student whose car is broken down or who is locked out or having trouble with her boyfriend, but really because it might be Danny, or someone about Danny. In our family the rule is: Anything can happen at any time. Period.

Mom picked it up. We heard her say, "Yes, we do know him. I had him in class a couple of years ago. One of those big lecture courses. Well, big for Krieger. And he's done some work for us. I believe you've met my daughter . . ."

I tried to get my mother's attention—what about me?—but she was facing the other way.

"That's right," she said. "Dorm parents. Not Andrew's. We're in Aster. West. Aster West." Mom was quiet for a moment or two and then cut off whoever was on the other end. "Why don't you come over," she said. "I understand. Right now would be fine.

"Sasha," she said, hanging up, "will you please set two more places. Andrew's parents will be joining us for dinner."

When you live in a dormitory with sad sack Tommy Mendoza and dopey Caroline Fleck and not-so-perfect Jillian Kramer, to say nothing of a three-legged dog who begs for chickpeas from the college salad bar, you are used to things changing suddenly. Even so, this was unusual: Andrew's very quiet parents were coming over for dinner. Why?

Jenny was telling us about a Dial soap commercial she had been in—"Those red toenails in the shower were mine," she said—when the doorbell rang. There stood Andrew's parents and behind them stood Andrew Hardy himself. "I checked myself out of the hospital," he announced cheerfully, though neither his mother nor his father looked very happy to hear it. His mother, in fact, looked like she had been crying. Her eyes and nose were all red, and she was carrying a handkerchief. His father looked even more angry than usual, but maybe he was just hungry.

"Sasha," Mom said, "please set another place at the table."

"Come in, come in," Daddy said, ushering the Hardys into the parlor as if they had been expected all along.

"We are very sorry," Andrew's mother began in her small, birdlike voice.

"Nonsense!" Daddy boomed. (Note: Daddy tends to boom when he is nervous and trying not to show it.) "Red wine, white wine, beer, cranberry juice, tomato juice, orange juice, seltzer?" he said, reeling off what seemed like the entire beverage section at the Krieger Safeway.

"Nothing," Andrew's mother said.

"Nothing," Andrew's father said.

"Well, come into the kitchen so you can meet our other

guest," Daddy said, and they dutifully followed him and he introduced them to Jenny, who had slipped back into her role as mother's helper and was wearing an apron.

"Jenny is an old family friend and a Krieger College graduate."

"And my teacher," I added.

Though she had only been in room 6B for three days, and though Mrs. B. had been there with her the whole time, I knew that Jenny Flum was going to have no trouble taking over. All those acting classes were coming in handy. She had a great Oh-yeah-you-can't-fool-me stare and an even better Hand-that-note-over-right-now-before-I-have-to-send-you-to-the-principal's-office glare. Also, she said that maybe, if we were good, we'd get to put on a play while Mrs. Blank was gone. With costumes and music and a party at the end.

"We must leave soon to Arizona," Andrew's mother said.

Daddy looked confused. "Aren't you staying for dinner? We thought you were staying for dinner."

"She doesn't mean now," Andrew's father said. "She means tomorrow. Our plane leaves tomorrow. Back to Tucson."

"Phew!" Daddy said. "We wouldn't want you to leave town without sampling the specialty of the house, chicken à la Abramowitz." And then the phone rang again.

This time it was Frank Benjamin, calling from the engineering lab. Something was wrong with his measurements, he said, and he needed me to measure Tripod's inseam. An inseam, in a pair of pants, is the distance between the crotch

(Note to myself: Learn to stop giggling when you say the word "crotch") and the bottom hem. In a dog, I guessed it was sort of similar, from the place where the skin kind of turns the bend and stretches from bone to bone, down to the toenails.

"Tripod's not here right now," I told Frank. "I'll call you back when she gets in."

25

Tripod showed up right as Mom was spooning the chicken "and all the fixin's," as Daddy likes to say, onto the plates. The dog barked once at the kitchen door and I let her in, and as I did I noticed that she had tomato sauce and strings of cheese in her beard.

"They're serving lasagna at the dining hall," I reported. Lasagna is one of Tripod's favorite foods, which practically everyone at Krieger knows. She's fond of chicken à la Abramowitz, too, just not the parsnips. In general, Tripod is not interested in root vegetables.

"Parsnips!" Andrew's father exclaimed when Daddy passed him a plate. "Almost no one cooks parsnips anymore!" Though he seemed genuinely pleased—how rare was that?— his wife, I noticed, was blushing. I was guessing that she was thinking something like "He's talking about me. I'm the one who never cooks parsnips," when Andrew confirmed it. "I've never had a parsnip in my life," he said.

"Me either," said Jenny Flum.

"That," Daddy declared, "is a travesty of justice." And then, turning to me, he said, "Do you know what that means, Sasha?"

"Well," I said slowly, "I think it means we'll be having parsnips at least once a week till I'm twenty-one." Everyone laughed, even Andrew's father, who, until then, I wasn't sure even knew how to laugh.

But he stopped almost as soon as he started and looked grave again. ("Grave" is a word Mrs. Blank gave us because she said she was afraid we'd grow up thinking it meant "dead," which it sort of does anyway, if you stretch the meaning.) He cleared his throat. It was clear that he wanted to say something. We all turned to look at him. He seemed uncomfortable.

"Thank you for taking such good care of Andrew." It took a second to realize the voice wasn't Andrew's father's; it was his mother's, and she was looking right at me.

"Yes," Mr. Hardy said.

"But we are not happy," Mrs. Hardy said.

"Oh no, can I get you something else," Mom said. "Some cheese and crackers. An omelet. Lasagna. I'm so sorry if this was not suitable."

Andrew's mother looked genuinely horrified. "No, no," she said.

"No, no," her husband said. It was as if the sound from her mouth had bounced off his and made an echo.

Andrew's father bowed his head slightly and spoke into his plate. "What Lucy is trying to say, I think, is that Andrew left the hospital against our wishes and against the wishes of his doctors. And now we are leaving tomorrow and there is nothing we can do about it."

"Wait a minute!" Andrew said. He put both hands on the table with such force that the spoons rattled. And now he, too, looked grave. I noticed that the bruise on his cheek was almost exactly the same yellow color as the chicken leg I was about to bite into, an observation that made me put it down. "I left the hospital for two perfectly good reasons. First"—he raised his index finger—"because I was feeling fine, was bored out of my skull, and needed to finish my schoolwork in order to graduate."

Personally, by my accounting practices, that was three reasons, but Andrew looked so serious that I didn't interrupt to tell him so. "Second," he said, and held up his middle finger next to his index finger. "Because it is too damn expensive and our health insurance won't pay for a hospital stay past today, so what is the point. You are already pissed off that I had to take out loans to pay for college."

Andrew's mother started to cry, and my mom put an arm around her. "Let's go into the kitchen," Mom said, and escorted her out of the room.

"Now look what you've gone and done!" Andrew's father said

angrily. Andrew looked down at his plate and speared a red potato. Jenny Flum looked down at her plate and speared an olive. I looked down at my plate and speared a piece of a parsnip.

"Look, parsnip, yum," I said, but no one so much as grinned.

"Kids these days!" Daddy said, trying to make conversation.

"Andrew is not a kid anymore," his father growled. "Andrew is twenty-four years old. I had already been in and out of the Navy at twenty-four. I was already married at twenty-four. I already had two kids at twenty-four. You'd better bet I wasn't hanging out at a place like this when I was twenty-four."

"You're twenty-four?" Jenny Flum asked Andrew.

"Yeah," he said. "I had to repeat a grade."

"Which one?" I asked.

"Tenth."

"You had to repeat tenth grade?" I was incredulous. And then, because I couldn't catch them, the words slid out of my mouth: "I thought you were so smart."

"He thinks he's so smart, too," Andrew's father said, but kind of quietly, and under his breath.

Andrew ignored him. "When I was a kid I went to a baseball camp run by Fritz Morton, the shortstop for the Cardinals. Then he got injured, retired, and ended up as the baseball coach for Merriweather Prep outside St. Louis. Fritz got me a scholarship to Merriweather, but the deal was that I would repeat tenth grade to get an extra year in with the Corps of Discovery—that was the name of the team, though everyone called them the Discos. And then I liked it so much that I stayed for a postgraduate year after twelfth grade even though I had already gotten into college."

Mr. Hardy made an unusual sound, something like a burp crossed with a sigh, and then a sour expression. "Aren't you going to say which college?" he asked bitterly.

Andrew fixed his gaze on the middle of the table where Jenny Flum's flowers sat in a clear Krieger College vase etched with the long, stern face of Erasmus Krieger. "Arizona," he said. "The University of Arizona. Where Mom and Dad wanted me to go."

"Because it was free," Mr. Hardy said bitterly. "One hundred percent free. Walk out of there a free man, no debts, and maybe a tryout with a major league club like—"

Andrew cut him off. It was obvious that this was an old argument between them. "But Fritz was eager to have me go to Krieger, where he had gone," Andrew explained to the rest of us. "He said, 'The baseball season is short, but the season for learning should go into extra innings.' "

Daddy, who might have been writing a poem in his head till then—he once wrote a sonnet to an onion between the salad course and dessert—perked up right then. "Fritz Morton was a poet of the first rank," he said.

"I didn't know he wrote poetry," Andrew said, turning toward Daddy. "Did you have him in class?"

Daddy laughed. "How old do you think I am? No, Fritz Morton was here before my time. But everyone who ever saw him play agreed he was the bard of the diamond."

"The bar of the diamond?" I said, confused. What was he talking about?

Jenny Flum (who, by the way, was looking at Andrew Hardy "with interest") and Andrew Hardy (who probably was doing the same in her direction; I couldn't tell, because his face, on my side, was so swollen) both laughed.

"Bard, Sasha," Daddy said. "Bard. As in William Shakespeare. You should know that."

"Oh," I said.

"Bard or no bard," Andrew's father said, "he's the one who did it."

"Did what?" Jenny Flum asked.

"Morton's the one who made Andrew turn down the baseball scholarship to Arizona and go into debt to come all the way out East to play for a bunch of losers. A tiny bunch of losers. And now this."

"He didn't make me do anything, Dad, except realize I wanted to come to a place like Krieger, a small place, where I can really get to know my teachers and—"

Mr. Hardy cut him off. "And where you have to do card tricks to earn enough money to pay your bills. At Arizona they'd probably have given you a car."

"I don't want a car," Andrew said.

"Who in America doesn't want a car?" Andrew's father

171

seethed. (Note: I love that word, don't you? Makes him sound like a snake.)

"Me," Andrew said.

Mr. Hardy turned to Daddy. "You're a smart man, Professor Abramowitz," he said. "Let me ask you a question: What kind of baseball coach convinces a boy *who has prospects*"—he shook his fist three times—"that baseball isn't everything?"

"A smart one," Jenny Flum said quietly, which caused Andrew to look at her gratefully.

"Okay, it's settled," Mom said, walking out of the kitchen, her arm still around Mrs. Hardy.

"Good!" Daddy boomed. (Note: I've already explained what it means when Daddy booms.) And then, after a minute: "Wait a minute. What's been settled? Was there a problem?"

"The problem," Mom began, "is that Andrew checked himself out of the hospital and Lucy"—she squeezed Mrs. Hardy's shoulder—"and Arvin"—she nodded in Mr. Hardy's direction—"are concerned about his health. So Andrew will stay here, in our guest room, and we'll keep an eye on him, make sure he doesn't chew his new cap, and call Neil if it's necessary, that sort of thing." She gave Mrs. Hardy's shoulder another squeeze, and Mrs. Hardy winced for a second before she smiled.

"This is very kind," she said. "Andrew will take his medicine?"

"Mom!" Andrew said, embarrassed.

"Oh, don't worry," Jenny Flum said. "Even though I'm

twenty-three my mom still reminds me to use toothpaste when I brush." Everyone (except Mr. Hardy) laughed.

"You're only twenty-three?" Andrew said. "I thought you graduated three years ago."

"I skipped seventh grade," Jenny said. "And also my birthday is in October, so I actually started school when I was four."

"Oh," Andrew said. Now it was his time to smile, but privately, to himself.

"The only wrinkle," Mom said, thinking out loud, "is this weekend. Even if Andrew is here, it's not like he can babysit."

"Oh, Mom," I said. "I'm eleven years old, which really means I've been alive almost twelve years. I don't need a babysitter."

"We are going away for the whole weekend, Sasha," Mom said firmly. "What if something happens and Andrew is too weak, or what if he has a relapse . . ." She didn't finish.

"I'm fine," Andrew said at the exact same time Jenny said, "I'll do it."

"What?" Mom asked.

"I'd be happy to come over and babysit Sasha," Jenny Flum said. "For old times' sake."

26

Andrew Hardy moved in that night. His dad and my dad walked over to Andrew's dorm and got some of his stuff. His mom and my mom made up the study—Danny's room when he's here. Jenny Flum, Andrew, and I hung out in the kitchen for a while before Jenny left. Andrew told her he'd show her some card tricks over the weekend. Jenny told Andrew she'd bring a tape of her Dial soap commercial. A couple of times I wanted to say, "Hey, guys, remember me?" because, truly, there were times when I wasn't sure they knew I was there. But then I decided it was kind of interesting, being a fly on the wall, but a fly who knows English and what it means, probably, when a twenty-four-year-old tells a twenty-three-year-old "It was really great to meet you."

That night, before I went to bed, I went into the study to say good night to Andrew, who, believe it or not, was going to sleep before me. He was lying in the bed my brother sleeps in when he comes to visit, the room my parents refer to as my brother's room. For a minute, maybe longer, I pretended that I was going in to say good night to my brother, and that my brother was not Danny but Andrew. And it seemed perfect. If Andrew were my brother, I thought, our family would be perfect. There would be Mom and Dad and Andrew and me, and we could live in a regular house and go out to dinner together sometimes and drive across the country and laugh at each other's jokes and tease each other without worrying that one of us might get agitated and do something crazy. There would be Mom and Dad and Andrew and me and we could have our picture taken and we could send it out at Christmastime (even though we're Jewish), and people would look at it and say "What a nice-looking family." Not nice-looking as in beautiful, but nice-looking as in nice. There would be Mom and Dad and Andrew and me, and Andrew would no longer have to wonder who his birth mother was, or worry that Mr. Hardy was always going to be disappointed in him for not becoming a professional baseball player, or at least trying, and Andrew would be happy, and I would be happy, and Mom would be happy, and so would Dad. He'd write a poem about it. It would be called "Portrait of My Happy Family."

27

Jenny Flum came home with me after school on Friday. That morning we had had a baby shower for Mrs. Blank. Each member of room 6B (except Mrs. B. and Jenny Flum) had contributed five dollars for a stroller with big wheels and black-and-white circles all over it. Mrs. Summers picked it out—looking at black-and-white pictures was supposed to make a baby smarter, I heard her tell Mrs. Blank—and made the refreshments (brownies, no nuts; brownies, nuts; blondies; lemon squares; snickerdoodles; gingerbread babies). At noon George—I mean Mr. Blank—showed up to whisk his wife away. Their plane was at four. We all lined up by the door and sang *"Adiós, Adiós, Hasta Luego,"* a Guatemalan folk song Mrs. Blank had taught us, then shook her hand, and Mr. Blank's, as they made their way toward the hall and—according to Mr. Baer, who gave a little speech between bites of snickerdoodles and lemon squares—"the rest of their lives."

When Mr. Baer, Mrs. Blank, Mr. Blank, and Pinky Summers's mother left, Jenny Flum walked to the front of the classroom, folded her arms, and gave us one of her looks. She was clearly trying out some technique they had taught her in acting school. She seemed to actually believe she could shut up twenty-two eleven- and twelve-year-olds just by staring at them. As she was staring us down, or at least trying to, Mrs. Blank rushed back into room 6B mouthing the word "Sorry," went over to the desk, opened the bottom left-hand drawer, and fished out the envelope with our nickname suggestions in it. She held it up as she walked toward the door, and said, "I'll let you know." We all yelled, "Bye, Mrs. Blank," again, and then she was gone. We could hear her shoes click-clicking down the empty hall.

"Well," said Jenny Flum, who was wearing a beige pantsuit with a black cotton sweater underneath. "Well." She trained her eyes on us again. One really cool thing about actors, I realized, is that they can take a little word like "well" and make it sound very big. Jenny Flum's "well" filled the room.

Jenny Flum said "Well" again when she got to our house that afternoon and saw Andrew, who was sitting in the kitchen eating cold leftover chicken à la Abramowitz. This "well," though, had a question mark at the end of it. She was asking how he was feeling.

"Not bad for a guy who just got up from a three-hour nap," he said, spearing an onion, which fell apart like a set of nesting dolls, one layer after another. "What about you two?" he asked, trying to piece it back together.

So we told him about the party for Mrs. Blank and about the black-and-white stroller and about the little gingerbread babies Mrs. Summers had made. We told him about the WELCOME HOME sign we made for Lindy that stretched from one side of the room to the other. We told him how, after lunch, Jenny Flum declared us "just good enough" to qualify to put on a play, with costumes and music and sets and programs—everything.

"What play?" Andrew asked, still struggling with the onion, which kept sliding off his fork.

"*Cheaper by the Dozen*," I said excitedly. "Which I've already read about four times. The book, not the play. Jenny wrote the play version."

"Jenny wrote the play?" Andrew said. "I'm impressed."

"Not really," Jenny protested.

"Don't be modest," Andrew said.

Jenny blushed. "I took this playwriting class when I was at Krieger and we had to adapt a book for the stage. I picked *Cheaper by the Dozen*."

"Cool," Andrew said.

"Jenny says it will work for 6B—that's our class—because there are so many parts. There are twelve kids to begin with, though Mary dies. By the way, where are Mom and Dad?"

"They left. This morning. You said goodbye. Remember?"

"Oh yeah," I said. (Note: I don't know about you, but sometimes I just completely forget what's going on *while it's going on.* Mom says that if you're distracted at any given time it interferes with something called "memory consolidation," which means, basically, that whatever you are doing does not "stick" to your brain. And the funny thing is that I had been distracted by the fact that Jenny, Andrew, and I were going to spend the weekend together, which meant that I could forget that Mom, Dad, and Danny were spending the weekend together, and that I, as a consequence, would be spending Monday afternoon with the Eraser.)

We talked about the play some more, with Jenny going on about her love of directing and Andrew volunteering to help her with the sets and me saying that I hoped I got a good part because in the last play we did, *Peter Rabbit*, I played a carrot. Afterward Andrew did five incredible card tricks for Jenny: Slap Happy, Predict-a-Pair, Only Time Will Tell, Spectator, and one whose name I can't remember,[6] all of which had her looking at Andrew like he was a genius. He didn't seem to mind.

"Wait a minute, I've got to get something," Jenny Flum

---

6. See Appendix 3 if you want to know how to do some of these and other card tricks.

said, and left the kitchen to go we did not know where. Nine minutes later she was back with a small paper bag from the Sugar Shack.

"Close your eyes and stick in your hand," she said to both of us, and I was really glad that Andrew pulled out the turkey drumstick ice cream cone, because in my opinion it never really tastes like real ice cream, plus the cone is always soggy, plus it is covered with nuts. I was even gladder that I got the ice cream sandwich, the standard vanilla ice cream chocolate wafer kind and not the new kind with strawberry and chocolate ice cream in addition to the vanilla. Just when your taste buds are used to, say, chocolate, you take a bite and your tongue gets a shock of strawberry (or "pink," as Carla says, as if pink were a flavor. No wonder she wanted to name her business Red).

We sat on the lawn in front of Aster, me, Jenny, and Andrew, eating our ice cream and watching two boys toss a Frisbee. The Cats were playing that afternoon, but it was an away game, so we couldn't go. Andrew seemed restless and tired at the same time.

"Why don't you do more card tricks?" I suggested, but he said no, five was the right number. He seemed a little sad.

Tripod wandered over then and plopped herself down between Andrew and Jenny and both of them began to stroke her coat and sometimes their hands would collide and they'd both giggle. Tommy Mendoza walked by with his new girlfriend, who had hair that was striped black-and-white like a zebra. Jillian Kramer, who was walking out of the building as they were walking in, laughed when she saw it. "Cool hair," she said to Tommy's girlfriend, who said, "Thanks."

"Watch out, Frank," Jillian yelled at Frank Benjamin, who was on his bike and about to run into her because he had just noticed Tripod and wasn't looking where he was going. "Oh, perfect, Tripod," he said, jamming on the brakes, which is when he almost ran over Jillian's perfect white sandals, "just the person I'm looking for." (Meaning Tripod, not Jillian.) He dropped his bike and wrestled himself out of his bulging knapsack, which he also laid on the ground. Then he stood up abruptly and took something wrapped in tinfoil out of his jacket, and held it out to Tripod, who also stood up abruptly, pushing aside Andrew and Jenny, who laughed.

"Lasagna," Frank said, unfolding the tinfoil. "I saved it for you."

While Tripod was devouring her treat, Frank reached into the knapsack and pulled out the thing that had been sticking out. It looked like a model of the Eiffel Tower, if the Eiffel Tower weren't completely straight but instead had a joint in the middle of it, and if the Eiffel Tower were upside down. (Or you were standing on your head.) "This is the structure for Tripod's leg," Frank said. "It's got microprocessors at the joint so that the action simultaneously mimics the action of the real leg. I've just got to try it on for size before we make it look more real." He looked around for Tripod, but she had snuck off as soon as she finished her lasagna. We called, but she didn't come.

"I think she's avoiding me," Frank said sadly, sticking the Eiffel Tower back in his knapsack and picking up his bike. "Tell her I'll see her later, okay?"

We said we would.

28

Mom called that night at nine thirty-eight, right on schedule.

"How is everyone getting along?" she asked.

"Two of us are getting along extremely well," I said, "and one of us is brushing her teeth and putting herself to bed."

"Good, good," Mom said hurriedly.

"How is it there?" I asked.

"We just finished the trust exercises and now there's a meditation. You know how I am with meditation." (Note: Yes, I did. For a while Mom thought it would be good for her—which meant good for her mind—to take up meditation. She bought a mat and a book and sat in the study chanting words that no one has yet discovered the meaning of for about an hour, three days in a row. On the fourth day she donated the mat to Tripod and told Dad that the whole time she was "meditating," she was actually thinking about all the things she could and should be doing, which made her more and more anxious, and that by the time the "meditation" was over, she was a nervous wreck.)

"How's Danny?" I asked.

"Good. Very good. Penny says he seems to have turned some kind of corner, though Daddy says it's probably because the Red Sox are up a game over the Yankees. We shall see."

We hung up then and I put myself to bed. In my dream it was Danny who had one leg and Danny for whom Frank Benjamin had built the upside-down Eiffel Tower. Danny put it on and Frank pushed the button to get it started and then, for the rest of his life, Danny was only able to walk in circles.

Jenny Flum was already in the kitchen when I got up the next morning. Andrew was still asleep. "What do you think he'd like better, Sasha, scrambled eggs with hot sauce, or an omelet, or pancakes?"

"Me!" I wanted to say. "What about *me*? What would *I* like best?" But I didn't. I said, "An omelet."

"I think I'll make pancakes, anyway," Jenny said, ignoring my suggestion. Not only was I being "left behind" yet again, as that *New Moon* article said might happen when your friend found "that special someone" and "that special someone" was definitely not you, I was being disappeared, poof! On the other hand, I, personally, if anyone would have cared to ask, would have preferred pancakes over omelets any day.

"Okay," Jenny said cheerily to herself (since I, apparently, wasn't there), "pancakes, here you come! Now, where would the flour be?" She opened a couple of cabinets and didn't find any. I watched her, playing dumb. She opened a few more. Nothing. Finally she turned and looked at me. "Sasha," she said, "do you know where your mother keeps the flour?" I considered not answering because, after all, I wasn't there, but then said innocently, "Flour?"

"Yes," Jenny said, "you know, that white powdery substance often used for baking."

"Look in the recycling bin," I said.

"The recycling bin?" Jenny said doubtfully.

"She keeps it there because it has a tight lid. No bugs," I said.

After the flour, it was the vanilla, the baking powder, the sugar, the measuring spoons, the mixing bowl, the griddle. She needed two eggs, I got her two eggs. She needed them beaten, I beat them. By the time the batter was made, I had done most of the work.

"Mmm," Andrew said, wandering into the kitchen wearing a gray Krieger Cats T-shirt, a pair of jeans, and a sleepy expression. "What smells so good?"

"It's the griddle. I'm making you pancakes," Jenny said proudly, and beamed. Andrew beamed back. I, on the other hand, walked out of the room. Jenny had said, "I'm making you pancakes." Not "we" are making you pancakes. I realize that if a person is invisible they shouldn't be able to be so angry, but I was completely and utterly furious. And hurt. And invisible. It didn't make exact sense, but it was the way it was. I went to my room. When we go on long car trips I always bring a pillow and a blanket and try to sleep so we get to where we're going faster. So I climbed into bed and slid under the covers and hoped the same thing would happen with this weekend.

No such luck. Someone knocked on my door about thirty-two minutes later. I didn't answer. More knocking. "I think she's asleep," I heard Andrew say to Jenny. "Sasha?" he said, slightly cracking the door.

I pretended I had just woken up. "Hmm?" I said.

"The Cats are practicing today," he said. "I thought we'd go over."

"But what about me?" I said.

Andrew stepped into my room looking very confused. "Like I just said. I thought we'd go over. To the practice."

"Oh, fine," I said, like I was doing him a favor, but secretly I was relieved that his "we" included "me."

In fact, his "we" did not include Jenny Flum. She decided to stay behind to work on the play.

"Did you bring your cards?" I asked Andrew when we were halfway to Twin Park.

"Nope. Not today. No cards, no glove, no cleats. It feels really strange."

When we reached the field, it took a minute for the team to see that it was Andrew. It was a little like walking in the

186

woods in summer. First the bugs don't seem to notice you, then they swarm.

"Hey, Hardy. Hey, An-drew. Yo, brother Andy. Attaboy, A.H." They were all over him, shaking his hand, slapping his back, slapping his butt (Note: I would not make this up), patting him on the head. I stood back and watched. It must be nice to have so many friends.

"Sasha, hi." I turned. The Ghost, Casper Wylie, was standing right behind me with his hand out. "Congratulations," he said. "We couldn't believe it when we heard that you were the one who basically figured out what was wrong with Andrew. That's amazing. You're like what, twelve?"

"Eleven," I corrected him.

"Whoa," he said. "Amazing. And that thing about the cap. That was just brilliant."

"The cap thing?" I asked, looking around quickly to make sure Andrew hadn't heard. "What cap thing? I didn't have anything to do with any cap thing!" I said loudly.

The Ghost looked confused. "Oh," he said. "But Andrew said you—"

"Andrew said?"

"Yeah, Andrew."

"You mean Andrew knows? Andrew knows? And he doesn't hate me?"

"Why should Andrew hate you?" Andrew asked, butting in.

"You were snooping!" I protested.

"The mark of a good detective," he said. "Why should I hate you?"

"Because of your baseball cap," I said weakly. "You really liked it."

"Sasha," he said seriously, holding on to both of my shoulders and shaking them a tiny bit. "Do you really think I liked that cap more than I like being alive?" He looked at me hard, and then in a flash a smile moved across his face like sunshine breaking out of the clouds on an overcast day. "Or more than I like you, you little rat fink."

Jenny Flum was gone when we got back. The note she left said: "Sasha, your parents called. They're coming back tonight. With Danny."

29

"So they all came back; what was that like?" the Eraser asked me Monday afternoon after I had settled into the worn leather patient's armchair across from his worn leather doctor's armchair.

"I don't know," I said. "Weird?"

"Are you asking me or telling me?" he said.

I gave him my best dirty look. "Telling," I said, studying his face. His nose was back to normal. No more redness and swelling. No more excess mucous membranes leaking out. (Note: Remember what Mrs. Blank advises about writing with detail.) It had been a while.

All of a sudden I had what I thought was a great idea, one of my best. "You should have a dog in here," I said. "A big friendly furry dog, like a golden retriever or a Bernese mountain dog."

"Would you feel more comfortable if a dog were here, Sasha?" he asked softly.

I shot him another dirty look. Why was everything, always, about feelings? "A dog would be nice," I said.

"I agree," the Eraser said, "but not everyone feels comfortable with dogs. Some people are afraid of them. And dogs, typically, shed. Even the ones with hair instead of fur give off dander. People are allergic."

"Then the allergic ones shouldn't come here," I said, and as I did, a light went off in my head: I'd convince the Eraser to get a therapy dog, I'd discover I had a terrible allergy to the dog, I would no longer be able to see the Eraser.

"What if people need me?" the Eraser was saying. "What if they have some sort of crisis—something happens—and then they can't come here because of the dog? It wouldn't work."

Case closed, he seemed to be saying, but I was unconvinced. I mean, who could need the Eraser *that much*?

"So back to Danny," he said. "Why was it weird?"

"They came home a day early," I started. "Well, not Danny. He wasn't supposed to come home at all. So that was weird. And then there was the whole fire thing, the fire at Trannell when almost everyone was off on a retreat, and since all the kids were already with their parents, the school just told them all to go home, not to go back to school, because the fire wasn't completely out, and it was the dorm that burned down, and no one knows if it was an accident or not. It's a big mess."

"And it's a big mess for you, too?" the Eraser tried.

"No. Not really. I mean Danny's home and all, but why should that be a big mess for me?"

The Eraser looked at me. I looked at him. The Eraser looked at me like I was telling a big fat lie. "What?" I said.

The Eraser stood up from his chair and stretched. "You are not going to like me saying this, Sasha, but I think you are angry. Pissed off." Then he sat down all at once and his leather chair sighed. Then he sighed. Then I sighed. The question wasn't "Was I angry?" The question was "Was I going to tell him?"

"It's just a little bit odd, having your brother, who you hardly ever see, just show up suddenly at your house, especially when there is someone else there, staying in his room," I admitted.

"I can see that," the Eraser said. (He does that sometimes— agrees with me, thinking that it will make me feel understood and more likely to share my feelings. Which in this case was true.)

"Because they didn't want Danny to get upset and because Penny, his counselor, says Danny does best with routines and when things don't change much, Andrew had to move out of the study, which is Danny's room when he comes home, even though Andrew is sick and just got out of the hospital, and now Andrew has to sleep on the couch in the parlor, under a creepy picture of Erasmus Krieger. It's disgusting."

"It sounds like you're angry because Danny displaced Andrew," the Eraser ventured. I ignored him.

191

"And then, the next morning, Danny wanted oatmeal for breakfast because they always have oatmeal for breakfast on Sunday mornings at Trannell, and even though Andrew and I both wanted waffles, Mom said no to waffles because she said she wasn't a short-order cook and was only going to make one kind of breakfast. Danny's kind. And in the afternoon Daddy, Andrew, and Danny went to see the Cats play, and I stayed home."

"You must have felt terrible not to be invited," the Eraser said.

"Oh, I was invited," I assured him. "I just didn't want to go with them." Daddy was Daddy—when the choice was between baseball and anything else, he'd always choose baseball. Danny was Danny—in this he was just like Daddy. And Andrew, he just didn't know. But I did. Going anywhere with Danny was always a risk. *Anything* could happen.

30

Play auditions began Tuesday. We were all going to get parts, Ms. Flum told us (Note: When she's my teacher, I'll refer to her as Ms. Flum. When she's my old babysitter or just about Andrew Hardy's girlfriend, I'll refer to her as Jenny Flum, or Jenny), and every one of us would get a good part, but she wanted to hear us read to know which part would be most suitable.

"Oh, Daddy, puh-leeeeese," I read, "puh-leeeeeese let me bob my hair and wear silk stockings." (I was supposed to be Anne, the oldest of the twelve Gilbreth children, trying to get her father to let her wear "modern" styles.) "I'll just die if I can't. Everyone in the whole entire eleventh grade has bobbed hair and wears silk stockings. It's already bad enough that we have red hair. I just don't see why we have to be different."

Ms. Flum posted the cast list on Friday afternoon. We all crowded around the bulletin board after recess, pushing each other, trying to get a look. "Bill," I heard one boy say. A girl's voice, "Martha." And another, "I'm Anne." But if I, Sasha Abramowitz, wasn't Anne, who was I? Ms. Flum clapped her hands. "Stop!" she yelled. "Sit down. Now." Her brow was knit and she looked mad. "My mistake," she said more quietly when we had all taken our seats. "I was under the assumption that this was not a sixth grade where the children don't know how to be courteous to each other but the self-controlled cast of a serious play." She glared at us. We all looked down at our feet. She walked over to the bulletin board and untacked the cast list. Before any of us had time to moan or whine or in any way object, she walked back to her desk. I was convinced, and I was convinced that everyone around me was convinced, that she was going to ball up that piece of paper, toss it into the garbage can, and tell us the whole thing was off. Class 6B would not be doing a play after all.

But we were wrong. She took the piece of paper and held it out in front of her and read it out loud. Carla was to play Ernestine, one of the older girls. Pinky was Tom Greaves, the Gilbreths' faithful handyman and sometimes cook. I was to be the mother, Lillian Gilbreth.[7] It was a pretty big part. The

___

7. Who, in real life, was this amazing woman? See Appendix 4, for my extra-credit report on Lillian Gilbreth.

next biggest part, in fact, after the father, Frank Gilbreth, Sr., the one who liked to parade all his kids through the streets of Montclair, New Jersey, in their car, Foolish Carriage, and ask bystanders, who seemed always to be pointing at them, "What do you think? Do my Chinamen or Irishmen or Frenchmen come cheaper by the dozen?"

But there was a mistake. A huge mistake. Ms. Flum had given the role of Frank Gilbreth, Sr.—the lead role—to James Schroder, a boy in our class who, as far as I could tell, had said nothing all year except "Here," at attendance. To say that he was quiet was like saying a jet plane is noisy at takeoff. Of course it's noisy, but it is more than noisy. James Schroder was quiet like that. And now he was supposed to play Frank Gilbreth, Sr.? What was Ms. Flum thinking?

"Listen up, people," Ms. Flum said before we could say anything. "I'm sure some of you are questioning some of my casting decisions"—she looked right at me—"and my advice to you is: Forget about it. Give it up. There is only one rule in acting—besides 'Try not to spit'—and the sooner you all learn it, the better off we'll be. Does anyone know what that rule is?" We all looked at her blankly.

"Okay, good. I'll tell you. The one rule is: The director is always right. Yes. The director is always right. Even if you think the director is wrong, the director is right. Always. Understand?" We said we did.

But James Schroder? He was the sort of kid that no one invited to a birthday party (except Mr. Nice Guy, Pinky Summers) because he never invited anyone to his. He was the sort of kid who was always called James, not Jimmy or Jamie or Jim, because he didn't have any friends who started calling him by a nickname that everyone else eventually called him by, too. (And, speaking of nicknames, we had just gotten a postcard from Mrs. Blank. She said that they loved all the nickname suggestions so much that they were having a hard time choosing. "George," she wrote, and then crossed out "George" and wrote "Mr. Blank is especially fond of" and then some name we couldn't make out because the handwriting had suddenly gotten shaky, probably from turbulence, somebody said.)

But James Schroder? That kid was going to have to have a personality transplant to play Frank Gilbreth.

Scripts were handed out that day and Ms. Flum said that she expected us to have our parts memorized within a week. Then she gave us one of her looks. No one said a word. We all knew better than to complain. The director is *always* right.

"You want to get together to practice on the weekend?" I asked Carla right after math.

"Your house or mine?" she asked.

"Yours," I said. "Danny is home." She knew what that meant.

"Mine's no good, either," Carla said. "Janice and my dad are redoing their bedroom and it's a noisy mess, and Janusz and my mom are cooking all day. They're doing that Krieger

Spices It Up! movable dinner, where people go from house to house eating foods from different countries. It's to raise money for something. I can't remember what."

"The rescue squad," Pinky said, coming up behind us. "My parents are doing it, too. My mom is making Thai lemongrass meatballs with peanut dipping sauce."

"So your house is out, too?" Carla asked.

"No, not really. We can go down to the basement. Mom made Dad insulate it with all this soundproof foam when he was trying to learn to play the fiddle."

So even though it had been my idea to get together with *Carla* to practice our lines, I found myself agreeing to get together with Carla and Pinky at Pinky's house at noon on Saturday. We weren't stupid. Show up at Pinky Summers's house at noon, expect to get fed by his mom.

31

At my house, Andrew was teaching Danny card tricks. And Danny was pretty good, too. He was focused and calm and could sit for a long time at the kitchen table counting cards, shuffling cards, laying them out by suit and by number. Whenever anyone stopped by because they were locked out of their room, Danny would do a card trick before handing over the key, with Andrew looking on and nodding encouragement. Frank Benjamin, who never locked himself out, stopped by every day anyway, just to see what new tricks Danny had learned. The Trannell fire, by the way, turned out to have been set by a former security guard who had gotten fired earlier in the year for sleeping on the job. His idea was to make it look like it was set by one of the students. The only problem was that all the students were away on retreat with their parents and their counselors. The damage was extensive.

Trannell would be closed until the fall. It was no longer a question *if* Danny would be home for the summer. He would be. He was.

Which posed a problem for Jenny Flum. She wouldn't come over if Danny was there. Which posed a problem for Andrew Hardy. He wanted to see her. Andrew was doing better, but he was still tired a lot of the time, which his doctors said was pretty normal for someone who had just had what Andrew had, and was susceptible to infection. They warned him to take it easy so he wouldn't have another "episode." Andrew was still going to classes, and doing his homework, and showing up at baseball practice (even though he couldn't play), and teaching Danny card tricks, and soon would be painting sets for our play.

"You need a time-motion expert in your life," Daddy told him, "like Frank Gilbreth, Sr."

Speaking of Frank Gilbreth, Sr., there he was, sitting on the couch in the Summerses' rec room, picking at a hole in his jeans, when I got there at noon on Saturday.

"I figured it would be better if there were four of us," Pinky said, shrugging. "Also, since James has the biggest part, he's going to have to practice the most." Typical Pinky, so thoughtful and nice you could almost hate him for being so thoughtful and nice—except that he was so thoughtful and nice that you couldn't, if you see what I mean.

Carla came down a few minutes later carrying a large tray

of pita bread sandwiches filled with chicken salad, plus choco-late cupcakes, plus a pitcher of lemonade with a bunch of lemon slices floating in it. " 'Just a little something to tide you thespians over,' " Carla said, quoting Mrs. Summers. "What the heck is a thespian, anyway? Where is Mrs. Blank when we need her?"

"Actor," James said quietly. " 'Thespian' means 'actor.' " His voice was deeper than I remembered it. Of course, the last time I heard him utter a sentence was what, second grade? James took a sandwich off the tray and immediately took a bite. Then he took another bite. Then another. (Note: I realize this is a common way to eat, bite by bite.) Four bites and the whole thing was gone.

"Your mom's a good cook," James said, taking another sandwich.

"It's just sandwiches," Pinky said. "No big deal."

"It depends," James said, but didn't say on what. He just shut right up. Typical.

We read through the script over and over again, trying not to look after a while when our own lines came up, which was hard. With a little prompting, James wasn't half bad. With a script in front of him, telling him what to say, he was just as talkative as anyone.

"I've got to go," Carla announced at twenty-one minutes af-ter two. "Piano."

The three of us tried to carry on after she left, but it wasn't the same. We had run out of steam. James and I packed up our stuff and said goodbye to Pinky and his parents, and found ourselves standing outside the Summerses' big house on Pine Marten Way.

"Well, bye," I said to James as I started to walk toward home. Without a word (of course) he started to walk with me. It didn't occur to me to ask him where he lived.

"How come you never talk?" I finally asked after five solid minutes of him walking alongside me and me listening to nothing but his footsteps and mine.

"I don't know," he said. "I guess I'm just out of practice."

"That's crazy!" I said. "It's not like you live on a desert island or anything." The spire of the Krieger chapel came into view, and then Krieger hill. I could see Tripod in the distance, trotting toward home. James didn't say anything, and I didn't say anything. Jillian Kramer was lying on a towel wearing nothing but a bikini, sunbathing—didn't anyone tell her about skin cancer? Three boys with guitars were sitting cross-legged under a tree, playing chords.

"Why, would you look, Lily, the children are all home," James said in his best Frank Gilbreth, Sr., voice.

"Why, Frank," I said, smiling, "I do believe you're right. Why don't you whistle for them." (Note: In the play and in the book, and in real life, too, whenever Frank "whistled assembly" all the children would stop what they were doing and come running.)

We had reached Aster and James was still with me and I wasn't sure what to do. "I'd invite you over, but I can't," I said, scrambling for some reason why I couldn't that didn't involve saying "because my brother is there."

"It's all right," James said. "It's no problem." But he looked sad, in the same forlorn way Tripod does when she stands outside the Krieger dining hall and no one even stops to scratch between her ears. (Which, to be fair, is not very often.) "But, um, Sasha, do you have, I mean can I, um use—" He couldn't seem to get the word out, and I didn't want to help him. I had this idea that if he couldn't ask to use the bathroom, I was safe from having to let him inside. But then he said it. What could I do?

"Sure," I said. "But my brother might be home," I added.

James looked at me oddly, and I had to admit, it did sound strange. How many people, at that very minute, were walking into houses or apartments (or igloos or yurts) where their brother was? Too many to count.

"My brother was at this school in Massachusetts and some guy burned it down, so now he's home," I said, hoping that would make it sound less odd.

"You mean Trannell Academy?"

My mouth dropped open. (Note: I realize that writers sometimes use this phrase to show surprise, and that it's just an expression and no one's mouth actually drops open. As for me, I was surprised. So surprised that my mouth really dropped open.) "How did you know?" I asked.

"It was on the news. They showed pictures. It looked real bad."

So he knew. James Schroder, of all people, knew about Trannell, about the fire, which probably meant he knew about Trannell itself, what kind of school it was. (In one of the reports I heard they called Trannell a "school for the emotionally challenged." Then they quoted the guy who set the fire, who said that they'd never convict him, since all the kids there were "touched in the head.") I took a deep breath and swallowed it quickly, like medicine I was hoping not to taste. "Danny has been at Trannell for three years," I said. "He's got this thing where . . . I mean, he's really smart. In certain things Danny is one of the smartest people ever. But he's got this thing where he sometimes says the same thing over and over, or blinks his eyes a lot or won't stop clearing his throat. It's really annoying and—"

"You mean Tourette's syndrome?"

I looked at him in amazement. Who was this kid? "I guess so," I said. Nobody has ever come right out and said that's what it is, but there are a bunch of books on Tourette's syndrome in our study, and I kind of figured out that's what it is. "How did you know?"

"Remember that biography project we had to do last year?"

I nodded. That's when I did my Eleanor Roosevelt report.

"I wanted to write about professional athletes who had disabilities but were still able to play at the highest levels. I ended up writing about a baseball player named Jim Eisenreich. He played for the Minnesota Twins and for the Phillies and the Dodgers and the Royals, and was in two World Se-

203

ries. He hit a home run in the '97 series when he was a Marlin. He has GTS—Tourette's syndrome."[8]

"I wonder if Danny knows about him?" I said, pushing open the door to our apartment.

"Does he like baseball?" James asked.

I laughed. "Does Danny Abramowitz like baseball? You should ask him that yourself."

---

8. See Appendix 5 for James Schroder's report on Jim Eisenreich.

32

James and I walked in on a typical Abramowitz family scene. Mom was in the parlor, sitting on the floor, under the gaze of Erasmus Krieger, surrounded by a ring of eight students who were also sitting on the floor. A huge poster of the human brain covered the floor between them, and as we walked by, a boy in shorts with really hairy legs was crawling near the top of it, shining a red pointer beam in front of him. "This is the cerebral cortex," we heard him say. "This is the cerebellum."

"Review session," I explained to James. "Mom teaches neuroscience. At Krieger. Obviously," I said, correcting myself, "since we live in a Krieger dorm."

Daddy was in the kitchen, sitting behind a wall of cookbooks piled on the table in front of him. "I'm looking for an ingredient," he said.

"Are you going to the Krieger Spices It Up! dinner, too?" I asked.

"What's that?" Daddy asked.

"Never mind," I said. "What are you making?"

"Nothing," Daddy said.

I looked over at James and shrugged. If he, too, had parents who sometimes acted like space aliens, he'd understand.

"It's that ridiculous crossword puzzle in *The New York Times*," Daddy said. "Every week I tell myself I'm not going to do it, and then, do I listen? I'm stuck at an eight-letter word with an 'R' smack in the middle that means 'red roux.' "

"What's roux?" I asked.

"How about 'marinara,' " James said quietly.

Daddy looked up and over the thicket of books and stared at James. "Why weren't you here an hour ago!" he said. "And who are you, by the way?"

"This is James, Dad," I said. "James Schroder. He plays Frank Gilbreth, Sr., in the play."

"See that!" Daddy said. "If I'd only consulted you earlier I could have saved a bunch of time. Bet you kids didn't know time grew in bunches, like bananas, did you? 'Marinara' it is." He wrote the word in, in pen. Daddy is very confident. ("When you find the right word you will *know*," he likes to tell his poetry students.)

James smiled, but didn't—you guessed it—say anything.

"Oh, the bathroom is over there," I said, pointing to

a blue door on which hung a sign that said VISITORS'
DUGOUT.

"Where's Danny?" I asked when I heard the lock slide shut.

A look of annoyance passed over Daddy's face like a single
cloud on an otherwise cloudless day.

"If you are worried that your brother is going to get in your
way or embarrass you—" he began. The toilet flushed.

"No," I said, cutting him off. "I just want to know where
he is. James wants to ask him a question."

Daddy continued to eye me suspiciously. Since Danny had
come home I had not once sought him out on my own.
"Daniel!" Daddy called, his eyes still on me.

Danny came out of his room, nearly colliding with James
coming out of the "visitors' dugout." "Sorry," James said.
Danny grunted.

"Danny," Daddy said, "this is James. He's a friend of
Sasha's. Sasha says he has a question for you."

"What," Danny said. "What question. James." His voice
was lower now, but still flat.

"Oh yeah," James said. "I did a report last year. Do you
know anything about Jim Eisenreich? The baseball player?"

Danny turned on the balls of his feet and took three steps
toward the refrigerator. Two steps past that and he'd be out of
the room. I looked over at James. He was staring at Danny's
back, looking confused. Before he could say anything (like
"Sorry if I said something to upset you"), Danny did a one-
eighty and came back toward us.

"James Michael Eisenreich," he said. "Born, 4-18-59, St. Cloud, Minnesota. 1982 to 1984, played for the Minnesota Twins, uniform number 4. 1987 to 1992, played for the Kansas City Royals, uniform number 22 and uniform number 8. 1993 to 1996, played for the Philadelphia Phillies, uniform number 8. 1997 to 1998, played for the Florida Marlins, uniform number 8. 1998, played for the Los Angeles Dodgers, uniform number 12. Career home runs, 52. Career RBIs, 477. Played in two World Series, 1993 and 1997. Hit a home run in the 1997 World Series for the World Champion Marlins. Highest salary, $1,650,000 in 1992. Rookie season batting average .303. Career batting average .290—"

"Danny," Daddy said, making the time-out sign.

Danny pretended not to see him. "Career season high, .361, batting for the Philadelphia Phillies in 1996. Salary in 1996, $1,200,000. Salary in 1997, $1,400,000."

Daddy tugged on Danny's sleeve. "Very good, Danny," he said.

"That's amazing!" James said. "How do you do that?" Nice—but the wrong thing to say unless you want Danny to start all over again.

Just then we all heard Mom say, "Who can explain the role of dendrites in memory formation?" and it dawned on me that she was holding her review session *in the parlor*. Yes, I know I saw her in there. Yes, I know that I had told James that that was what she was doing. But it wasn't *what* she was doing, it was *where*. In Andrew's room. But where was Andrew? And more to the point, where was all his stuff?

"Where's Andrew?" I asked suddenly, looking around.

"Do you have another brother?" James asked.

"No, he's a friend."

"An-drew Har-dee. An-drew Har-dee," Danny said, rocking back and forth.

"Andrew Hardy the baseball player?" James asked. "Wow. That's amazing."

"Well, it's not like he doesn't go to Krieger," I said, annoyed. Why wasn't anyone answering *my* question? Andrew Hardy could at that very moment be back at the Krieger Community Hospital and would I know? No.

"Where is Andrew?" I demanded.

"Cool it, Sasha," Daddy said. "Andrew decided to move back to his dorm room. He said it would be easier to study for finals there."

And easier to see Jenny Flum, too, since she was determined not to have anything to do with Danny Abramowitz ever again, which meant, among other things, never coming over.

I know this is mean, and I know it does not, as Mom and Dad like to say, "speak well of my character," but I was jealous of Jenny Flum. I mean, why did she get to make the choice never to see Danny Abramowitz again—and, more to the point, why didn't I?

The kids in Mom's class were standing and stretching, and suddenly a wave of them washed into the kitchen looking for the snacks Mom had left for them there, and coming to say hi to Daddy, and the room filled quickly with their bodies and their voices. It was a happy, energetic sound, like bees pollinating a flower bed, which is why I didn't hear it at first. Not "it," actually, but "him." Danny. Clearing his throat, over and over again. Clearing it like someone who was just about to say something, but then didn't say something, he just kept on clearing his throat, except that nobody knew that he didn't have something to say and they all got quiet and looked at him and he just kept making that noise in the back of his throat, and when Mom said "Danny," in a low, sharp voice, he started to say terrible words, over and over again—embarrassing, awful, terrible words. I couldn't bear to look at anyone's face. I knew theirs would mirror my own. And then the door to the outside, to freedom, was opened and the class filed out without a word while Mom kept saying "Danny, stop," and Danny didn't.

And then it was just Danny and me and Mom and Dad and James Schroder standing in the kitchen, Mom with her hands on her hips looking shaken, Daddy telling Danny that he had to apologize, Daddy begging Danny to apologize, and Danny pacing and muttering and biting his hand, and James just looking and looking, his eyes moving from one person to the other, to every person, it seemed, except me. And what was I supposed to do? I felt like running out of there and never going back. Running far from home and far from Krieger, and far, especially, from James Schroder, who knew more about the Abramowitz family—the ugly, awful, miserable Abramowitz family—than anyone should have to know.

"I'm sorry," Danny mumbled. He was still biting his hand.

"I'm sorry what?" Daddy said.

"I'm sorry Mom," Danny said. "I'm sorry Mom. I'm sorry Mom. I'm sorry Mom."

"Enough," Daddy said.

"Oh no!" James said, pointing suddenly to the clock. "I have to get home. I'm going to be late." His voice sounded panicky, like he had already done something very wrong.

Mom turned toward the sound of his voice with a surprised look on her face—startled, I think, to realize there was someone else in the room, someone who was not one of "us." "Would you like to use the phone?" she asked.

"No," James said. "I, um, can't. Sasha, can I borrow your bike?"

"Sure," I said, "but—"

"Where do you live?" Daddy asked. And when James named an address on Erasmus Boulevard, Daddy said, "We'll give you a ride."

"Wait!" Danny yelled. It was a big banshee yell and it stopped all of us, every one of us, in our tracks.

"You want to know something else about Jim Eisenreich," Danny said. And then, before any of us, especially James Schroder, who was about to be later than he already was, could even so much as blink yes or no, Danny said, "James Michael Eisenreich, born 4-18-59, has Tourette's syndrome, just like me."

Mom looked at Dad, Dad looked at me, I looked at James, James looked at Danny.

"I know," James said. "I know that."

33

Wish #1: That my brother was normal.

Wish #2: That I could say "My brother has Tourette's syndrome" as easily as Danny said it today.

34

School had become the play and the play had become school. From the time the morning bell rang, till after the dismissal bell in the afternoon, it was play, play, play. (Note: That's "play" as in "theater," not "play" as in "swing set.") Some of the parents complained to Mr. Baer that "the substitute in room 6B was neglecting the curriculum"—according to Jenny Flum, who told Andrew Hardy, who let it slip to me—but what could he do, now that Mrs. Blank and George—I mean Mr. Blank—had run into problems in Guatemala, something to do with Lindy's vaccinations—according to Jenny Flum, who told Andrew Hardy, who let it slip to me in the same conversation mentioned above—and wouldn't be back for the rest of the school year. Jenny Flum and *Cheaper by the Dozen* were here to stay and hallelujah to that!

Most of us had learned our lines by the end of the first week. Or, more accurately, most of us had learned most of our lines. On the playground during recess you could see clusters of kids from room 6B gathered together, practicing. Walking to school, we practiced. On the school bus, we practiced. During gym. At lunch. We were no longer sixth graders, Ms. Flum told us, we were a theater company, the 6B Players. And we liked it, all of us, even the kids who had never liked school before, or had goofed off, or had been invisible. Like James.

Only we didn't call him James anymore, we called him Frankie. Carla had started it, and it just caught on, and now James was gone and a tall boy with a shy smile who, blessedly, never mentioned that afternoon at my house to me or to anyone else, had taken his place. He'd say, "Well, Lily, you'd better ask Tom Greaves what's for lunch." (Which meant "I wonder what Mrs. Summers has packed in Pinky's lunch box today?") And "Lily, you would use less energy if you stopped flapping your arms" (which he'd say when I was stumbling over one of my lines). But then one day, while we were walking home from school, he said, "Your brother likes the Red Sox, doesn't he?" It was less than two weeks till showtime and James was coming over to practice our lines totally off-book. (No scripts. We had left ours in our lockers on purpose, so we wouldn't be tempted.)

I said that Danny did. Daddy, too. "Basically, they're fanatics," I said.

"Well, you know that ballplayer Jim Eisenreich I told you about?"

"And then Danny told you about," I added.

James/Frankie smiled. "Exactly," he said. "Well, you know when it was that he realized he really had a problem?"

"When he tried to blow up the family swimming pool by threatening to pee on a pile of pool chemicals?" I asked.

James/Frankie looked at me strangely but went on. "*In Fenway Park!*" he said emphatically, as if it were the punch line to a joke or the solution to a puzzle. "In Fenway Park, where the Red Sox play. It was when he was with the Twins and they were playing Boston and he had these tics and he didn't know what the heck was going on; he just couldn't control what his body was doing although he was an amazing player, but in the middle of the game he just couldn't go on, the tics had gotten really bad, and he was scared, and he didn't play again for three years. The Royals bought out his contract from the Twins for a dollar. One dollar."

"Uh-huh," I said. Why was he telling me this? What was the point?

James/Frankie suddenly looked embarrassed. Like he had said too much. Like maybe I wasn't going to like him anymore. Like maybe he'd have to go back to being regular old invisible James.

"I thought Danny would think it was interesting," he said cautiously, "because it happened at Fenway." And then almost in a whisper: "And I thought you would think it was interesting, too, Sasha, because it has such a happy ending. Seven years after the Royals picked up his contract for a dollar, the guy slams a three-run homer in the second game of the World Series. 1993. When he was on the Phillies. It's not like he didn't still have Tourette's."

All of a sudden I began to feel my blood boil. It began down in my feet and moved swiftly up my body till my head was pounding and my eyes were swollen in their sockets and my heart was beating in my chest like an African war drum. "You don't know anything! Why don't you just butt out! Why don't you mind your own business. Did it ever occur to you that maybe I don't want to talk about this?" I shouted, and pushed past him and started to run up the hill toward home, leaving James standing there, getting smaller and smaller, which is just how I wanted it to be. "Good," I thought. "Good, good, good, good."

"Sasha, want to see a new card trick?" Danny asked as I stepped inside.

"No," I said, and went into my room and slammed the door.

"It's called The Wizard Takes a Holiday," Danny said from the other side.

"No," I said. "N-o. Just leave me alone. Alone. A-l-o-n-e. Get it, moron?"

I stayed in there for a long time. At first I just cried. Tears poured out of my eyes. It wasn't fair, I told myself. It wasn't fair that I had to have a brother who was so different, who had problems that other people felt like they had the right to discuss out loud in public. But what if I didn't want to discuss it with them? What if I didn't think it was so interesting that Jim Eisen-whoever had some kind of breakdown at Fenway Park instead of in my own backyard? And what if I *did* think it was interesting, what did that story have to do with Danny, or with me, or with the rest of our lives? Because that was the thing: no matter what, Danny was always going to be my brother.

That was the first hour. The second hour was different. The second hour I felt even worse.

It was as if, having emptied out all my horrible thoughts about being Danny's sister, I had room to think horrible thoughts about me: What made me think I was so perfect, and how could I have been so creepy to James/Frankie when he'd only been trying to be nice and a real friend. Just the thought of that made me cry again, but just for a while, and then I got calm and just lay there thinking about James Schroder, thinking about how he had reached out to me and to Danny, and about how he must be feeling now. Which got me out of bed and into the kitchen, where Danny was trying out The Wizard Takes a Holiday on Mom, and Daddy was cooking. (Not chicken à la Abramowitz, but spaghetti with red roux.)

"Has anyone seen the phone book?" I asked.

No one had, which was pretty common. Students would

come in and borrow it and forget to give it back. Then we'd have to call the phone company and they'd bring over a couple more and then those would disappear. And now they were gone again.

"What are you looking for, sweetie?" Daddy asked gently. He knew I had been in my room crying. How could he not? It was written in red lines and splotches (my own personal Morse code) all over my face.

"I need James Schroder's phone number," I said.

"Forget one of your lines?" Daddy said.

"Sort of," I replied.

"Oh, just call Information," Mom said. "It's not your fault we don't have a phone book."

So I dialed Information and asked the operator if she had a number for Schroder, in Krieger, and she said there was no regular listing for Schroder in Krieger.

"Are you sure?" I said.

"Let me check the computer again," she said. I could hear her fingers tapping on a keyboard. "Well," she said after a while, "I do show a TTY line for a Schroder on Erasmus Boulevard. Please hold for the relay number."

"Dad," I said, putting my hand over the receiver so the operator wouldn't hear me, "what's a TTY line?"

But she heard me anyway. "It's a special telephone line for deaf people," she said.

35

I waited for James on the corner of Erasmus and Main from seven in the morning till quarter to eight, thinking that he'd have to walk through this exact intersection in order to get to school. All night long I'd practiced what I was going to say to him, how I was going to apologize.

But he never came. School bus after school bus went by, and more cars than I could count, and men in business clothes on bikes, and kids on scooters and skateboards, and plenty of people on foot, but none of them James Schroder. I had to run to get to school before the late bell rang, and I came in hot and panting and needing a trip to the water fountain, which Ms. Flum granted, but reluctantly, because, she said, we were in the final stretch and needed to focus all of our energies on the play, not on ourselves. Coming back into the room, I glanced quickly in the direction of James's seat, expecting it to be empty. Why would he come to school now—now that I had been so mean to him? But he was there, in his regular seat, and when he saw me looking at him he waved. It was just a casual thing, a slight tilting of the pencil in his hand, but I saw it: he waved. I smiled at him gratefully (though I don't think he knew that) and sat down.

Confession: I hate it when kids pass notes in class. First of all, because teachers seem to think the best way to stop kids from writing notes is to read the notes out loud, which means that anyone, at any time, can be completely humiliated. Second, because kids know that and write mean stuff that they want read aloud—stuff like "Katie Harris should know better than to wear a tankini in the pool," and "How many times a month do you think Mark Savitz brushes his teeth?" And third, when it's not mean stuff like that, it's stuff that is supposed to make other people feel left out.

That said, I decided to write James Schroder a note anyhow.

"Dear Frankie," I wrote quickly at the top of a piece of notebook paper, shielding it with my hand so no one could see. "Dear Frankie." I looked at those words and considered my options. I could write "Sorry I was such a jerk," or "I'm so sorry I yelled at you and ran away," or "Thanks for telling me that about Jim Eisen-whoever." The last seemed the best, but it was also the least direct. I put down my pencil and crumpled the paper. Writing, I decided, was the coward's way out. I was just going to have to talk to him. And, anyway, Ms. Flum was going around the room asking each of us how many of our friends and relatives would be coming to the evening performance because she needed to tell the custodians how many VIP rows to leave in the auditorium and how many tables to set up in the cafeteria for the cast party. Pinky said six, because his grandparents were coming, and Carla said twelve, because all of her parents were coming and they were each bringing both of their parents, and I said three, the basic Abramowitz unit, and James said none. "None?" Ms. Flum repeated, and James nodded his head, and she went on to the next person.

There are probably all sorts of good reasons why the sixth grader who is the star of the sixth-grade play would have absolutely no one come to watch the play for which he had given up countless Saturday mornings and afternoons after school, the play in which he had more lines than anyone—but I couldn't think of any. It bothered me that I couldn't, bothered me the way a mosquito bite does—I couldn't help scratching it, and the more I did, the more it itched. And then, in the middle of practice—Act 1, Scene 2, as Frank is lugging a huge Victrola upstairs to the boys' bathroom so they can learn French (Note: It's a long story. I suggest you read the book)—I had what may be the third most important thought of my life so far: The reason no one was coming to hear James Schroder become Frank Gilbreth, Sr., was because they couldn't. Hear, that is. They were deaf.

I had to tell someone, but who? We were all onstage, in costume. Only Ms. Flum wasn't up there. She was sitting in the auditorium looking up at us, clipboard in hand, taking notes about the things she wanted to tell us later, all the little mistakes we were making. So I walked off the stage. I knew it was wrong. I knew she was going to be furious that I was stepping out of character, but I had to. I was by her side before she even noticed I was missing from the scene.

"Get back up there, Mrs. Gilbreth," she said so everyone could hear.

"Jenny, I have to talk to you," I said quietly.

"Get back up there, Mrs. Gilbreth," she repeated.

"But I need to tell you something important. About James," I insisted.

Ms. Flum ignored me. "Understudy," she called. "Who is Sasha's understudy?" And right then, in front of everyone, she took my part away from me. Not forever, she told us. Just until I understood that actors don't just wander off the set "to chat."

I sat there in stony silence. I sat there through scene after scene as my understudy tripped over my words. I sat there after everyone else had gone backstage to change. I sat there till, finally, Ms. Flum came over to me and said, "Well, Sasha, what was it that you couldn't wait to tell me?" I didn't like the way she said this. It was like she was certain that whatever I had to say couldn't have been very important at all, and I seriously considered saying "Forget it," or "Nothing," and just walking away. If James Schroder didn't have anyone coming to the play, that was his business. But I didn't do this.

223

"You know when you asked us how many people were coming to the play and James said none?" I asked. Ms. Flum nodded. "I think I know why."

Ms. Flum looked at me curiously. "Why?" she said.

"Because they are deaf," I said.

"Both of them?"

"I don't know. He didn't tell me. I figured it out."

The kids were coming back from the dressing room, streaming across the stage and down to where I sat talking to Ms. Flum. Everyone wanted to know what it was that I had been so desperate to tell her.

"It's private," she said. "Ask any more questions and the whole play will be performed by understudies from the fifth grade, understand?"

36

That afternoon when I got home from school there was a message waiting from Jenny Flum. The same Jenny Flum I had just left half an hour before, in the gym, painting the last flats with Andrew Hardy. "Can you meet us, alone, at the Cats game this afternoon?" she asked. Alone, I figured, meant no Danny, no Carla, no Pinky, no James/Frankie. Us, obviously, was Jenny Flum and Andrew Hardy. I left a hasty note for Mom and Daddy, walked out the door again, and ran into Frank Benjamin.

"Sasha," he said, "have you seen Tripod?"

"No," I told him. "I just got home."

"I finally got her to let me near her with the new leg, and then she growled and ran away." He looked sad and a little bewildered.

"Sorry, Frank," I said, hopping onto my bike. "If I see her I'll have a talk with her."

"Thanks," he said. "I mean I already got an A on the project, but it would be really nice to see the leg in action."

Jenny and Andrew were already at Twin Park when I got there, Andrew in a clean Cats uniform with a brand-new Cats cap.

"You're not playing, are you?" I asked.

Andrew laughed. "What are you, my mother? No, I'm not playing. Maybe Saturday. Saturday is the last game of the season. The last game when I will suit up as a Krieger Cat."

"Saturday is also the play," Jenny said. Dress rehearsal was the day before, during school. The big performance was Saturday night. There were signs all over town announcing it.

I looked around, worried that maybe Danny and Daddy would be at the game, too, but then I remembered that this was the afternoon that Daddy was taking Danny to see the Eraser. Ever since that "episode" in the kitchen, the one when James was over, Mom and Dad thought that maybe Danny's medication needed adjustment. The Eraser was supposed to help with that.

"Listen, Sasha," Jenny Flum said, "I'm really glad you figured this thing out about James's parents. I'm not sure I'm supposed to be telling you this, but since you were the one who told me, I think I can tell you that you're right. Both of James's parents are deaf."

226

"I told you . . ." I began, feeling triumphant, but then the meaning of what she was saying started to sink in. "Both of his parents?" I said.

"Yes," she said. "I guess it's not uncommon for deaf people to have hearing children."

"Does James know sign language?"

"Probably," Jenny said. "I don't know for sure. But probably, if his parents do."

"No wonder," I said.

"No wonder what?"

"The first time I ever really talked to him I asked him why he didn't say much and he said he was 'out of practice.' Now I see what he meant."

"So I have this plan," Jenny Flum said, and then she laid it out for Andrew and me, and it was really good. Really, really good. And if you think I'm going to say what it is, here, now, guess again. You are not going to know until James knows, on Saturday night, the night of the performance.

37

Everyone was in the audience, and I mean everyone. Mom and Dad and Danny were there, of course, and all of Carla's parents and all her grandparents, and Pinky's family, and Frank Benjamin, and the entire Krieger Cats baseball team, including Andrew Hardy, who had played the last three innings of the very last ball game of his college career, hitting a double and a single. All the seats in the auditorium were taken—we could see that when we peeked out from behind the thick velvet curtain that was the only thing that stood between the 6B Players and fame, or, more likely, between the 6B Players and total, utter humiliation.

We all said we weren't nervous, but I think we all were. And then the music started, and we took our places, and my palms got cold and sweaty and I looked over at James, who had one of those "How did I get myself into this in the first place?" kind of looks, and I smiled at him as much as I could get my muscles to move on command, and he did the same, and then the curtain went up. James, who was wearing a brown-and-black-striped three-piece suit, stepped to the front of the stage, pulled a pocket watch from his vest pocket, put a yellow whistle in his mouth, and blew. Children came racing in from all parts of the stage and lined up in rows on either side of him, in order of height, tallest to shortest, boys on his left, girls on his right.

"Not bad, not bad," he said. "Seventeen seconds.

"Tell me, Lily, what's the record?"

I stepped forward. I was wearing a black dress with tiny white dots that looked like snow at night and a black hat and carrying a white purse. I opened the purse and took out a small notebook. I flipped a few pages and stopped.

"Nine seconds on May the twelfth," I said and snapped the notebook shut with, according to Ms. Flum's advice, "authority."

It was at this point in the play that James was supposed to harrumph, tell the kids how disappointed in them he was, trick them into believing he was really angry, and then give the boys pocketknives and the girls nail clippers and let them climb all over him and swing from his arms as if he were a jungle gym, telling him how wonderful he was. Instead, he saw *her*. And once he saw her, he saw *them*. And once he saw them, he closed his eyes. And once he opened his eyes, he was okay.

She was Jenny Flum. She was standing off to the side of the stage, in front of the open curtain, wearing a white blouse, white pants, and white sneakers, and making broad gestures with her arms, kind of like she was dancing. But she wasn't. She was signing. Jenny Flum knew sign language. She had learned it that semester she interned at the National Theatre of the Deaf.

They were James's parents. They were sitting in the fourth row—his father, a thin man with dark hair, his mother, gray-haired, a little overweight—and they were looking at Jenny Flum at the same time that they were looking at their son, the star of our play. Jenny Flum had called them and arranged for them to be there. Andrew had picked them up in my mom's (clean) Honda after Jenny called to tell him that the coast was clear: James was with me in Dad's (filthier than usual) Honda, on the way to the school.

I looked at James and hoped he wasn't angry that no one had told him—that it had been a surprise. I hoped he was happy. His parents, when I caught a glimpse of them, looked happy. Happy and proud. But of course I couldn't say anything about it to him because I wasn't Sasha right then, I was Lillian Gilbreth, the mother of twelve children, one of whom, in the most dramatic moment of the play, was soon to die of diphtheria. And then, in the middle of a scene, when Ernestine, Martha, and Anne were demonstrating Frank Gilbreth's amazing touch-typing technique, James Schroder gave me the answer to the question I couldn't ask. Though it wasn't in the script, though our director hadn't given her approval, he reached over and took my hand and gave it a squeeze.

38

I don't know when I first noticed that Andrew Hardy was no longer in his seat. It may have been the last scene of the first act, when all the little kids show how fast they can do square roots, or the second scene of the second act, when everyone has ganged up on Frank Gilbreth, Sr., even his wife (me), and voted to buy a dog for five dollars. At some point I saw that Andrew's seat was empty, and when I looked again, through the bright stage lights, expecting to see that he had returned, he still wasn't there.

As for Danny, I know exactly when it was. Act 2, Scene 4, when Frank, Sr., is chaperoning his daughters on dates, a completely hilarious scene that James was really hamming up. But then Danny, in the audience, started to ham it up, too, echoing what James was saying till some of the people sitting nearby told him to shush. I saw Daddy stand up and take him by the wrist and walk him out the door. And then, a few minutes later, I saw Daddy come back and take his seat, and the play continued to the end. The curtain came down, the applause was deafening, the audience was standing up, cheering, we took our bows, first the whole cast, then the individual members, and when James Schroder came to the front of the stage, the place went wild. It was so loud that there was no way, absolutely no way, that Mr. and Mrs. Schroder, who were standing and clapping, too, could fail to hear it.

We all cheered for Jenny Flum, and for ourselves, and then the curtain fell for the last time and we all stood there, listening to the final round of applause, not wanting it to end, not any of it, until Mrs. Summers, who was in charge of refreshments, stepped up to a microphone and invited family and friends to the cast party in the cafeteria, and we all raced off to the dressing rooms to get out of our costumes.

The cake Pinky's mom had made stretched the length of one cafeteria table and was in the shape of a Pierce-Arrow, the kind of car the Gilbreths drove. Pinky said she had gone to the library to research it so it would look authentic. And it did. As much as a cake can look like a car. Especially a cake with the name of every single member of the cast and crew written on it in red icing. James was already in his regular clothes when I got there, talking with his parents and Jenny Flum—talking with their hands. They were all smiling and James's mom, who turned out to be very short, had one arm around James at the same time she was using the other to sign. I wanted to go up to them and say hi—I was, in a way, responsible for them being there—but I suddenly felt too shy to interrupt. It seemed so private. But then James saw me and excused himself and came over to where I was standing waiting for Mrs. Summers to cut me a piece of cake—preferably a wheel, I told her, which had the most icing.

"My father made this cake," James said.

"No he didn't!" I said indignantly. "Mrs. Summers did." Okay, it was great that he was a star, great that his parents were there, but why did he have to brag about something that was just untrue?

"Really," James said. "Here, ask him," and he pulled me in the direction of his parents and Jenny.

"This is Sasha," James said, both with his mouth and with his hands, "Sasha Abramowitz." I watched to see how he was going to make "Abramowitz" with his hands, expecting lots of crazy, jerky gestures and circles around his ears, but he just mouthed it, slowly, and they responded and everyone laughed except me.

"What's so funny?" I asked. It was an odd feeling, not knowing what people were saying.

"Dad said that you made a good wife," James said, coloring. Then he signed something to his father, and his father signed something back, and then his mother got in on the conversation, and so did Jenny Flum, and I just stood there, looking from person to person, totally shut out, and it occurred to me that ordinarily this was what it must be like for James's parents.

"Okay, okay," Jenny Flum said, "here's the story: Pinky's mom had the idea for the cake, but her oven wasn't big enough to bake it. When I first got in touch with the Schroders, Mr. Schroder told me he probably couldn't come to the play because he's the night manager at Ruserl's Bakery downtown. As soon as I found that out, I arranged for the cake to be made there. It was done in five pans, and then Pinky's mom iced the whole thing together. So it was really a collaboration."

"Your father is a pastry chef?" I asked James.

"He works in a bakery," James said modestly.

"Tell him I want to be a pastry chef when I grow up," I told him. "In addition to being a writer. And tell him the cake is delicious."

"Where's Andrew?" I asked Jenny while James was signing to his dad.

"I was just wondering that myself," she said, craning her neck to look around the crowded room.

"Do you happen to see my parents?" I asked Jenny. It had just occurred to me that though I had the second lead in *Cheaper by the Dozen*, neither of my parents had come to congratulate me, let alone take my picture. In my imagination they were on the other side of the room, trying to get to me, but couldn't, since they were constantly being stopped by people who had to tell them how good I had been. More probably they were out in the hall with Danny, calming him down. Trust Danny Abramowitz to steal my moment of glory.

"I don't," Jenny reported. "I'm going to scout around."

But then it turned out she didn't have to. There was my mother, standing on a chair holding a glass, which she was tapping with a spoon. (Plastic, so it wasn't too effective.) I got ready for the inevitable toast—the thank-you to Jenny Flum, the thank-you to the people responsible for the cast party, and, of course, the thank-you to the cast for such outstanding commitment and talent. Mom clinked, and though it took a while, everyone quieted down.

"I'm sorry to interrupt you," she said. "Something has happened." There was a gasp in the room, as if everyone had inhaled at once, and suddenly the quiet got even quieter. "Many of you know our son, Danny. Danny Abramowitz. Danny is missing. He left the play in the second act because . . ." She paused. I could feel every drop of blood in my body rushing to the surface and my face burning as if I was out in the brightest sun. And I was, wasn't I?—"Because he sometimes can't control his movements or what he says. We know he was outside for at least part of the second act and that Andrew Hardy, the Krieger student who built all the sets, was out there, too. Andrew is also gone. If anyone has seen them, or thinks they know where they may be, please come tell me."

She stepped down from the chair and the room remained silent. The only sound came from James Schroder as he explained to his parents why our party was suddenly and

236

abruptly going to break up. Because it was. Parents started gathering their kids and ushering them out the door as if, if they stayed a minute longer, something about Danny would rub off on them and they, too, would be tainted. Within minutes the only people left in the cafeteria were the custodians, Jenny Flum, Pinky, his mom, dad, and grandparents, Carla, Cliff and Janice (Janusz had driven the others home earlier so they could watch the whole play over again on video), me, James Schroder, his parents, and the Krieger Cats.

(Note to the Eraser: Would you like to know how I felt then? Mad. Mad, mad, mad, mad, furious. First Danny almost ruins the play, then he ruins the party, now he'd ruined my life. Attention! Attention, everybody, Sasha Abramowitz has a brother who can't control himself. Attention, attention, everybody, in case you haven't noticed, Sasha's brother is a freak.)

I found a chair, sat down, and put my arms on the table in front of me and buried my face in my arms. If people wanted to think I was scared and worried about Danny, fine, but that wasn't it. I just wanted to disappear.

After a while someone tapped me on my shoulder. I looked up and it was James and he was holding a flashlight. "The police said it's too soon to file a missing-person report, so Carla's father says we need to try to find them ourselves. Everyone's split into teams and is going out to search. It's nine-thirty now. They're keeping the school open. We're supposed to report back at eleven."

237

"So?" I said.

"So you're on my team," James said. "Actually, you are my team. Doug Jacoby, the Cats' catcher, was supposed to go with us, but I think he got confused and left with a different group. We're supposed to walk from here to your old house and back."

"Great," I said unenthusiastically. "Just great." But I did stand up and I noticed, as I did, the condition of the cafeteria. (Have you ever read *Great Expectations*? If you haven't, you should. It's by Charles Dickens—one of my dad's favorite authors, even though he's not officially a poet—and in it there is this woman, Miss Havisham, who was supposed to have gotten married about a hundred years before but then she gets jilted and the wedding never happens and her room becomes this place where time stands still. She's still in her wedding dress, with one shoe on, and there's cake and all the preparations for guests. That was what this was like.) The cake was half-eaten, with the knife stuck in it in mid-slice. Baby carrots and slices of red pepper were resting in dip. Opened bottles of soda still fizzed. Everything had been left as if there had been a fire drill. As if there had been a fire drill and everyone would be coming back any minute now.

But it was just me and James, our footsteps echoing down the hall and out the door where the shock of night air made me shiver.

"This is stupid," I said. "We are never going to find them."

James ignored me. "If you were Danny, where would you go?"

"If I were Danny, I'd go to the South Pole and never come back," I said. "But I am not Danny. I am Danny's sister. Lucky for me."

We walked in silence then, slowly, James poking behind hedges and shining the flashlight into the tops of trees. It felt like we were going inch by inch, stone by stone, and getting nowhere.

"Let's just try to think like Danny would think," James tried again. There was a bus stop ahead and he sat down and I sat down next to him. Somehow, out of nowhere, a bus arrived, and the driver opened the door and light from the bus streamed out like water released from a dam. An old man got off the bus and the doors sighed shut again and it moved on.

"Maybe he got on a bus," James said. "Maybe he got on a bus and is spending the night going around and around Krieger."

"Maybe," I said doubtfully. It was as good an idea as any, but I didn't think so. That was the weird thing. I felt like I could tell if Danny was around, like my body could tell me, the way some people can walk a piece of property and know where there's water in the ground. I didn't *feel* like he was on a bus, any bus.

"Let's go to my old house," I said. I didn't want to say anything and jinx it, but I could see Danny there. Danny and Andrew. Danny saying, over and over, "This is where she was, this is where she was," meaning Jenny Flum—only Andrew wouldn't know that.

39

"James," I said as we walked along, "what is it like to live with them? With your parents?"

"You mean because they're deaf?"

"Well, yeah," I said, trying to sound casual, though it made me uneasy, asking that question, like just asking was kind of prejudiced. But James didn't seem to mind.

"I don't really know," he said. "I mean, they've always been my parents. I learned to sign before I learned to talk. I guess I was a really late talker and they were worried that I was deaf, too, which is odd, when you think of it, them being worried that I was deaf, but they were. And then this social worker said that maybe I was resisting, which is how I ended up getting sent to see this guy, Dr. Serkowsky, which really helped."

"You?" I said. "You see the Eraser, too?"

James looked confused.

"The Eraser. Dr. Serkowsky. I have to see him, too."

"I don't see him anymore," James said. "It was when I was younger. He's the one who made me understand that it was okay to talk and be part of the hearing world, and that I wasn't betraying my parents. Because, as a little kid, that's what I thought. He made me realize it was okay to be different from my parents, and that it was okay for my parents to be different from other kids' parents, and that being okay is not the same thing as being easy." He stopped and laughed. "And now I'm talking too much," he said.

We were in front of Mrs. Mendelsohn's. Her yellow Lincoln, the same yellow Lincoln, was sitting in her driveway. Her curtains were drawn. I tried to "feel" for Danny. And for Andrew. I tried to be open and empty so I could fill up with their presence, if they were around. I stood still, and put my arms out, and felt . . . cold.

"We should cut through the yard and look at our old pool," I whispered to James. I didn't tell him about the image in my mind, of Danny, not flipping or flopping, but Danny, face-down, floating.

We pushed back the hedge of lilacs Daddy had planted when I was born, which was thick now and delicious, and stepped into my former backyard. "The pool is over there," I said, pointing. Only it was not. The pool was gone. In its place was grass, a whole lawn of it, upright and still.

40

We walked back to the school defeated, meeting others along the way whose luck had been no better than ours. In our absence the cafeteria had been turned into a mobile command center with Cliff Smith at the helm. He had a map of Krieger tacked to the wall and a list of routes that searchers had taken. He had coffee and cake. He had the entire Krieger Cats roster, minus Andrew. He had Jenny Flum.

Jenny Flum. As soon as I saw her my stomach began to hurt. Leave it to Danny Abramowitz to destroy what should have been one of the best nights of her life. She must hate him, I thought. She must hate me. If it weren't for me, Danny wouldn't have been at the play. If it weren't for Danny, Andrew would still be here. But he wasn't. He was gone, and the trail was cold.

———

At 11:03 Cliff Smith announced that my parents were on their way to the police station and the search was being put on hold till the morning. "It's too dark; we're too tired," he said. It wasn't an especially chilly night, he said, and if Danny and Andrew had to sleep outside somewhere they might be cold but they wouldn't be in danger. Jenny Flum began to cry, so Cliff stopped talking and started to wrap up the cake so it wouldn't get stale overnight.

"I guess we'd better go home," I said to James. "Cliff will give us a ride."

I was exhausted. I'm sure James was, too. The play in which we had leading roles seemed as far in the past as being four years old. Because I no longer felt like a child. I can't say I felt like a grownup, either. But whatever it was that had, that very morning, let me live my life without even considering what it must *feel* like not to be able to hear music or the sound of your baby laughing, or what it must feel like to be that baby, growing up, or what it *did* feel like to have every single person in school know something about your family that you didn't even want to know yourself—whatever that blankness was, it was gone. There was so much more I wanted to ask James about his family, but Cliff was there and I was tired, so very incredibly tired, and as soon as I climbed into the backseat I fell asleep.

The next thing I knew, Cliff was stopping the car and turning off the engine and saying, "Sasha, wake up. We're at the hospital. They've found Andrew. And Danny."

41

If you are like me and your brother is like Danny and your best friend's father wakes you up in what feels like the middle of the night from a dead sleep in the backseat of his car, a backseat that has no other passenger in it but did when you got in (how many minutes, how many hours ago?), and tells you you're at the emergency entrance to the Krieger Community Hospital, you know, without anyone saying anything, that something has happened to Danny. Maybe he was hit by a car, maybe he has hurt someone. Maybe he has hurt himself . . . Whatever it is, you also know that Andrew Hardy has saved him, that Andrew Hardy is the one who got him here.

"Where's James?" I asked groggily as Cliff led me across the parking lot, which was lit, I noticed, by orange streetlights that hummed.

"We took him home," Cliff said. "That's when I found out."

For some reason, maybe sheer exhaustion, maybe because I didn't want to know yet, I didn't ask him what it was that he'd found out. Whatever it was, it was not good. That was for certain.   .

The bright hospital lights, as we walked in, reminded me of standing onstage looking out at row upon row of upturned faces—faces I knew were there but had to strain to see because the lights made a wall that separated me from them. The lights made a wall here, too, but this one was curved at the top like a canopy and made a tunnel so bright it made me squint. There was no choice but to walk through it even though I had no idea where it led, or if, when I turned around, it would allow me to go back to where I'd been.

A nurse directed us past the admitting desk to a different corridor. "You want to be in purple, then orange; watch for the color of the chairs," she said, which, in the middle of the night, sounded like code, or a foreign language, or both. Cliff was holding my hand. His wedding ring was cold and cut into my finger. I was going to ask him to loosen his grip, but then I realized it was me—I was the one who was holding on so tight.

We turned a corner, and then we turned another corner, and out of a silence I hadn't really noticed until it began to lift, I began to hear voices, five or six, seven or eight, highs and lows, yet none of it distinct. It was just sound. And then, above all these, I heard someone say, "This one is called The

Four-Ace Extravaganza." Danny—it was Danny's voice. And the voice of the person who said, "Show me"—that was Jenny Flum's.

I really woke up then, startled and alert, which is not to say that I was any less confused. Here was Danny, sitting in an orange plastic chair in the Krieger Community Hospital. Here was Jenny Flum, sitting next to him. Here was Raja Williams. Here was the Ghost, and Doug Jacoby. Here were my parents, huddled with Dr. Neil Levine. They waved when they saw me, and my mother held out her arms. "He's going to be okay," she said, though she didn't sound sure. "He's going to be okay," she said again, with even less conviction.

"He's out of surgery. They removed his spleen," Dr. Levine explained to me. At least, he thought he explained to me.

"*Who* is out of surgery?" I demanded.

They all looked at me with a mixture of surprise and alarm.

"Andrew," Daddy said. "Andrew Hardy. I think it is fair to say that Danny saved his life."

42

I have now heard the story of how Danny Abramowitz saved Andrew Hardy's life so many times that I feel as though I was there. Which of course I wasn't. I was up onstage, mothering twelve and then eleven little Gilbreth children. Andrew, who had taken his last college exam that morning, had gone over to Twin Park in the afternoon. He was feeling good. A little tired from having studied hard for his math test, a little sore from moving sets the day before for Jenny Flum, but basically good. He was in uniform, it was the last game, the continuation of the one that had been suspended when he got hurt, and he couldn't resist. He decided to play. Just an inning or two, if it went that long—that's what he told himself. But when he got a double in his first at-bat, and a single his next time up, he told himself that maybe, just maybe, if he stayed in the game they could win.

Andrew left at the top of the thirteenth inning. He had promised Jenny Flum he'd be at the theater early, to help with the programs and, as she put it, to calm her nerves. So he ran from the ball field back to his room, changed, and rushed over to the school, forgetting to eat lunch, forgetting to eat dinner—not that he noticed. But by the time Andrew had settled into his seat and the lights went down and the play began, he was feeling a little dizzy. His head began to hurt. He left the auditorium and went outside and sat on the school steps. That's where Danny found him.

Danny had had to leave the play because he was acting up. Danny was supposed to stay outside, on the steps, till the play was over. If he did that, Mom said, he could come inside for cake. If he didn't, Daddy said, there would be consequences.

Andrew was not doing well. His head hurt and then his nose began to bleed, and wouldn't stop. Then Andrew rested his head on his arms, which were folded across his knees, and Danny didn't know if he was asleep or if he was dead. He put his arm on Andrew's back and felt that he was still breathing. He knew he had to do something. But here was Danny's dilemma: if he went back inside to tell someone, Mom and Dad would know he had left the steps and *there would be consequences*. And so he decided to get Andrew to the hospital on his own, without telling anyone, which is what he did. He picked Andrew up and carried him. Not all the way, but till he saw a taxicab and flagged it down. Andrew got to the hospital around 9:17 p.m., just about the time the 6B Players were taking their final curtain call. But he wasn't officially admitted for *almost two hours*, which is why no one knew he was there.

43

The diagnosis was that Andrew had had a relapse. He had overdone it, he had not really followed doctor's orders, and now he was going to have to stay in the hospital while they figured out if he needed bone marrow and, if so, who the donor would be. Andrew was going to miss graduation and he was going to miss the annual Reunion Day baseball game, when old Krieger Cats like Fritz Morton came back and played against the current Cats team. Danny was going to throw out the first pitch.

"Sasha," Andrew said softly from his hospital bed the first time I went to visit him after the splenectomy. (Note: Definitely not on anyone's vocabulary list till medical school. It's the operation where they take out the spleen. The spleen, Dr. Stackpole told me, is one of our internal organs, but I guess one that we can spare.) "Sasha Marie Curie Abramowitz, I owe you an apology. I lied to you."

I looked at Andrew. His skin was the color of goose eggs. He had lied to me?

"Remember when you asked me about my birth mother, about trying to find her?"

I nodded.

"Remember when I said it didn't matter?"

I nodded again.

"I was just saying that. It wasn't true."

"How come?"

"Because things are okay the way they are. And because I was scared."

Andrew got quiet, so quiet I thought he had fallen asleep. But then he raised his head off the pillow and said, "But things are not okay. Obviously." He pointed to the I.V. stand behind him.

"Sasha," Andrew said, "if you're still interested, when I get better I'd like Drew Hardy and Associates to help me find my birth mother." He stuck out his hand. We shook on it.

44

I'd like to end this here by telling you that in their last game, the Krieger Cats won 10–0 and that Raja Williams pitched a perfect game. That Casper Wylie, the Ghost, hit a grand slam. That Andrew Hardy's RBIs clinched the first win of the season. But I can't.

I'd like to say that the Cats won 7–2 or that it was 3–2, but no. The actual score, after fourteen innings, was 1–0. The Cats went down fighting. They were valiant.

Jenny Flum says she will assign "valiant" as a vocabulary word next week. In the meantime, I think I will define "valiant" like this: As my brother, Danny, getting Andrew Hardy to the hospital (even though he knew there would be *consequences*); as my parents, for loving Danny *no matter what*; as Andrew Hardy, for deciding to search for his birth parents; as

James Schroder, for learning to speak; as Tripod, our dog, for letting us know that she didn't need four legs to be whole; and as me, Sasha Marie Curie Abramowitz, nine spiral notebooks and fifteen gel pens later, for hearing the voice calling across a crowded room like a friend, and writing this book.

Appendixes

Eleanor Roosevelt (1884–1962)

by Sasha Abramowitz

Eleanor Roosevelt's first name was not actually Eleanor, it was Anna. Anna was also the name of her mother, who died when Eleanor was a child. Eleanor and her brother were raised by their grandmother because, two years after their mother died, their father died, too, and they became orphans. Even before her parents died, Eleanor had an unhappy childhood. Her mother, who was very beautiful, made fun of her because she was so plain-looking. Her nickname for Eleanor was "Granny."[1]

Eleanor married her cousin Franklin Roosevelt in 1905. President Theodore Roosevelt, Eleanor's uncle, walked her

---

1. Russell Freedman, *Eleanor Roosevelt: A Life of Discovery* (New York: Clarion Books, 1993), p. 5.

down the aisle. Eleanor and Franklin had six children, though one died when it was a baby. At the start of their marriage, Eleanor mostly took care of babies and went to parties. When Franklin was elected to the New York State Senate in 1910 they moved from New York City to Albany. Eleanor didn't have time to do much except raise her children, but during World War I, when Franklin became Secretary of the Navy, she got involved with the Red Cross.

That was really the beginning of the *real* Eleanor Roosevelt, the one who was so well known and who was involved in lots of activities and organizations like the League of Women Voters. When her husband got polio in 1921 and was paralyzed, she helped him become Governor of New York and President of the United States by traveling around the country, talking to people, and reporting back what she was seeing. Eleanor cared a lot about poor people and about ending racial prejudice. She started a furniture factory near her house in Hyde Park, New York, to help people who were unemployed. She encouraged Franklin to write laws that made sure all people were treated equally.

Eleanor Roosevelt was a very popular First Lady. She had her own radio program, and a newspaper column called "My Day." Later, after her husband died, she served as one of the first United States delegates to the United Nations, where she helped write the Universal Declaration of Human Rights.

She wrote books, traveled around the world many times, and had a television show whose first guest was Dr. Martin Luther King, Jr.[2] She died in 1962 at the age of seventy-seven. Four presidents attended her funeral.

2. Freedman, p. 1.

Report on Marie Sklodowska Curie

by Sasha Marie Curie Abramowitz

Marie Curie was born in Warsaw, Poland, on November 7, 1867. Her parents, Bronislawa and Wladyslaw, named her Manya Sklodowska. She changed her name to Marie when she went to college at the Sorbonne in Paris. Marie's mother died when she was eleven, and the family was very poor. There was not enough money to send her to study in Paris, so she had to work as a governess for many years. She also taught poor children for free in her spare time. Marie wasn't able to begin her studies in Paris until she was twenty-four years old.

At the Sorbonne she studied physics and math and graduated first in her class in 1893, which was doubly amazing because when she started she hardly spoke French, and also because she was one of the few women studying science there. In 1894 she met Pierre Curie, who was a physics professor and inventor.[3] They got married the next year. Their first daughter, Irène, who grew up to be a famous scientist herself, was born in 1897. Their second daughter, Eve, was born in 1904. She was the only person in her family who did not win a Nobel Prize.

Not long after Irène was born, Marie Curie decided to go back to school to study for a doctorate in physics. She wanted to find the cause of mysterious rays she had observed being emitted by an element called uranium. According to a profile of Marie Curie called *Woman of Courage*, "within two months she had made two important discoveries: the intensity of the rays was in direct proportion to the amount of uranium in the sample, and nothing she did to alter the uranium affected the rays. This led her to formulate the theory that the rays were the result of something happening within the atom itself, a property she called radioactivity."[4] Working with her husband, Marie then discovered a method for removing the radioactive material, which they called radium.

Marie Curie got her physics doctorate in 1902. (She was the first woman in Europe to get a doctorate in physics.) The

---

3. Pierre Curie and his brother invented the piezoelectric crystal, which is still used in electronics today. Pierre himself came up with the Curie Point, which shows that the magnetic properties of a substance change according to its temperature. (Mollie Keller, *Marie Curie* [New York: Franklin Watts, 1982], pp. 27–28.)
4. "Marie Curie, Remarkable Scientist: a *Woman of Courage* profile (www.northnet.org/stlawrenceauw/curie.htm).

next year she and Pierre won the Nobel Prize in Physics. Tragically, three years later, Pierre was run over by a horse-drawn wagon and killed.

Marie Curie went on without him. She was given her husband's job at the Sorbonne; it was the first time a woman was on the faculty there. She continued to work on radium and another radioactive element, polonium (which she named after Poland, where she was born, and which she missed terribly). In 1911 she received a second Nobel Prize, this one in Chemistry, for this work. She was the first person ever to get two Nobel Prizes.

When Irène Curie grew up, she began to work with her mother in the laboratory, using radioactive materials to take "pictures" of the body. In other words, they helped develop X rays. This was important during World War I. They helped set up X-ray machines on the battlefield so soldiers could be helped right there.

While we know that X rays and radiation are dangerous (that's why they put that heavy apron on you when you get X-rayed at the dentist's office), the Curies did not. Marie Curie often handled radium with bare hands. She started to get sick when she was in her fifties, and over the next decade it got worse. She was dizzy all the time, heard ringing in her ears, and went blind. She died of aplastic anemia on July 4, 1934, the year before Irène Joliot-Curie and her husband, Frédéric, won their own Nobel Prize for Chemistry. Marie Curie had overcome a lot of obstacles in her life, like the early death of her mother, the family's poverty, and the fact that she had so little to eat when she was a student in Paris that she fainted in class,[5] but aplastic anemia was one obstacle that even she could not get over.

5. Keller, p. 22.

Appendix 3

CARD TRICKS *All card tricks adapted by Andrew Hardy. Used by permission. Thanks to Margaret Stratton, Sarah Stratton, and Sophie McKibben for their help with these.*

Back Flip

The Trick:

Back Flip will demonstrate your ability to make cards move on their own.

How It's Done:

1. Shuffle the deck a couple of times in full view.

2. Fan out the cards and ask a spectator to pick a card.

3. While she or he is looking at it, put the deck back together, and quickly, without anyone noticing, move the top card of the deck to the bottom of the deck, flipping it faceup. Then, also quickly and without anyone noticing, turn the whole deck over so that card is on top. You will now be holding a deck where only the top card is facedown, but you will be the only one who knows this.

4. Ask the spectator holding the chosen card to slip it back into the deck.

5. Say "Hocus-pocus" and spin around on your feet once. While doing so, turn over the top card so it's no longer the only card facing down, then turn the whole deck over so that card is back on the bottom.

6. Fan out the cards again, and the chosen card will be the only card showing its face.

The Jacks' Party

The Trick:

In this trick you will separate four sets of cards from the deck—the kings, queens, jacks, and aces—and then, as if by magic, bring them back together again.

How It's Done:

1. Ask for a volunteer to assist you. Have her or him stand next to you. Then, while removing the kings, queens, jacks, and aces from a pack of cards, tell your audience that you have a story to tell them.

2. Put the remaining cards from the deck aside.

3. Start the story, saying, "The jacks decided to have a party." Then deal out the four jacks, faceup, in four separate piles.

4. Continue, saying, "The first guests to arrive were the kings." Deal out the four kings, faceup, on top of the four jacks.

5. Then say, "The queens arrived a little later and brought lots of loud music and their dancing shoes." Now deal out the four queens on top of the four piles.

6. "Oh no!" you say. "The neighbors must have called the police." Deal out the four aces, one to a pile. Say: "The people at the party are being arrested for disturbing the peace."

7. You will now have four piles of cards, each with an ace, king, queen, and jack in it.

8. Put the piles on top of each other so they make one pile with sixteen cards in it.

9. Look at the audience and say something like "This is bad. This is *very* bad. The police cars have crashed into each other."

10. Turn to your volunteer and say, "I need you to cut these cards directly in half. It is very important that you make the cut directly in the middle of the pile." Hand her or him the pile. Tell the volunteer that it's fine to cut the cards a couple of times.

11. Take the pile back from the volunteer.

12. Deal the first four cards from the pile facedown on the table, left to right.

13. Then deal the next four on top of those, and the next four on top of those, and the final four on top of those. You will now have four piles of cards, with four cards in each.

14. Say something like "Phew!" and wipe your brow. "Even though they got all knocked about in the accident, they managed to arrive at the police station"—pause as you turn over each of the four piles—"all together again!"

15. Show the audience that all the jacks are in one pile, all the kings in another, all the queens in the third, and all the aces in the fourth.

This trick will work every time as long as *the pile of cards is cut right in the middle, according to step 10.*

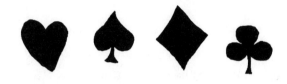

The Four-Ace Extravaganza

The Trick:

This trick allows you to find all the aces in the deck magically.

How It's Done:

1. Before you start, and without anyone seeing, remove the four aces and put them on the top of the deck.

2. Then remove the cards 2, 3, 4, 5, 6, 7, 8, and 9 of any suit and put these cards on top of the aces, in order, so that the top card is the 9. Again, make sure you do this in advance without anyone seeing.

3. Ask a spectator to pick a number between 10 and 19. While she or he is thinking, shuffle the deck, making sure

that the first twelve cards stay in order on the top. *(This is very important.)*

4. After asking the spectator to name the number, count that many cards, one at a time, into a pile on the table.

5. Ask the spectator to add those two digits together and state the sum. Put that many cards back into the pack from the pile, starting with the card on the top.

6. Remove the next card from the pile and place it faceup on the table. It will be the first ace. Set it aside.

7. Place the remaining cards from the pile back on top of the deck and shuffle again, making sure that those cards stay on top in order.

8. Ask the spectator to name a number between 10 and 19 again, then repeat steps 4–7.

9. Repeat step 8. You will now have found three of the four aces.

10. Place the deck facedown in front of the spectator and ask her or him to think of a number between 1 and 8. Have the spectator count that many cards, facedown, onto the table, from the top of the deck.

11. Turn the last card he or she dealt out, faceup.

12. If the number he or she thought of is 9, the card turned over will be the ace and the trick will be over. If the number

is not 9, the card turned over will be one of the number cards (from 2 to 9).

13. In this case, ask the spectator to deal off that number of cards from the pile, counting the turned-over card as the first card.

14. Much to everyone's amazement, the last card she or he deals will be the fourth ace!

Only Time Will Tell

The Trick:

In this trick you will read the mind of an audience member by picking a single card from the entire deck that he or she has chosen while your back is turned.

How It's Done:

1. Ask a member of the audience to shuffle a pack of cards and, while doing so, to think of one of the four suits.

2. Turn your back to the audience and ask the participant to remove all the cards of that suit from the deck except for the king.

3. Ask the participant to lay all the cards out on the table as if they made a clock face, with the queen at twelve

o'clock, the ace at one, the two at two, and so on. (The jack will end up at eleven o'clock.)

4. Tell the participant to look at the clock and think of a particular hour—for example, five o'clock—and to keep that time to her- or himself.

5. Now ask the participant to collect the cards, starting with the queen and going counterclockwise, so the ace is on the bottom, and to put this pile on top of the rest of the deck.

6. With your back still turned, ask her or him to recall the time she or he thought of before, and to count out that many cards from the bottom of the deck and put them on the top of the deck.

7. Turn around.

8. Ask the participant to deal out the cards, one by one, in random piles, all over the table. Keep a close eye on her or him as she or he does so, counting as the cards are laid out. The thirteenth card will be the one thought of, so make sure you know where it is, but don't let on that you know.

9. When all the cards are laid out, look them over, then turn over the thirteenth card.

10. Your audience will be amazed!

The Wizard Takes a Holiday

The Trick:

This trick will convince your audience that you have ESP.

Preparation:

Shuffle a deck of cards and, as you are finishing, secretly glance at the top and bottom cards. Then ask a spectator to assist you.

How It's Done:

1. Spread the cards facedown on the table and tell the spectator that you are going to predict the card he or she will pick.

2. Remembering which card was on the bottom, say that card. (E.g., if the bottom card was the 5 of clubs, say, "I predict you will pick the 5 of clubs.")

3. Tell the spectator to point at the card on the table he or she thinks is that card.

4. Pick up that card, mutter something like "Nice job," but do not show it to anyone. Let the spectator think he or she picked the right card. Hold on to it. (Let's say that the one picked was really the 8 of spades.)

5. Now tell the spectator that you predict he or she is going to pick the card just selected. (In this example, it's the 8 of spades. That is, say, "I predict that the next card you choose will be the 8 of spades.")

6. Ask the spectator to point to another card from the table. Pick it up without showing it to anyone and say "Nice job" or "Good work" again. Hold on to this card, too. (Let's say it was really the 3 of hearts.)

7. Now say, "I will be picking the final card myself, which, I predict, will be the 3 of hearts."

8. Remembering where the bottom card is, pick it up and put it in your hand. You will now be holding three cards. (In our example, the three cards are the 5 of clubs, 8 of spades, and 3 of hearts.)

9. Shuffle the three cards.

10. Ask the spectator to tell you which cards you predicted would be picked. As she or he says each one, take it from your hand of three and display it.

Extra-Credit Report on Lillian Gilbreth

by Sasha Abramowitz

Lillian Gilbreth was the mother of Anne, Mary, Martha, Frank, Jr., Lillian, Bill, Jack, Jane, Bob, Ernestine, Dan, and Fred Gilbreth, and the wife of Frank Gilbreth, Sr. They were all characters in *Cheaper by the Dozen* and *Bells on Their Toes*, two books about the family written by two of the Gilbreth children, Ernestine and Frank, Jr.

Lillian Gilbreth was born in 1878 and lived ninety-three years. Her parents were rich, and they expected that when she grew up she'd get married to a rich man, stay at home, and raise a family. Well, she did get married and raise a family, but first she went to college, at the University of California, where she did so well that she was the first woman in the history of the school to give the commencement address. Then she went to graduate school in English literature at Columbia University, but she had to leave and go back to the University of California because the professor she was supposed to study with at Columbia refused to lecture to women. After graduation, she went to Europe. Her ship was sailing from Boston, and before it did she was introduced to Frank Gilbreth, Sr., a Bostonian who ran a construction company. They got married in 1904 and decided to have a dozen children.

Even though Lillian had a lot of babies to take care of, she continued her education. In 1915 she received a doctorate in psychology from Brown University. Frank, who had never gone to college, asked her to study psychology because he thought it would be helpful in the business they ran together—Gilbreth, Inc. Gilbreth, Inc., gave advice to companies about how to become more efficient.

When Frank Gilbreth, Sr., died in 1924, Lillian took over the business and the family. Before this she was more in the background. (She didn't put her name on any of the books she and Frank wrote together because she thought businessmen wouldn't take them seriously if the books had a female coauthor.) Once Frank died, though, she began to give seminars on worker efficiency in her home, and to lecture at colleges and businesses all over the world. In 1926 she was the first woman to become a member of the American Society of Mechanical Engineers. Later, she became the first female engineering professor at Purdue

University in Indiana. She helped design efficient kitchens and appliances. Think of her every time you step on the pedal of a flip-up trash can or when you are using an electric mixer. Lillian invented both of these. She died in 1972.

Report on Jim Eisenreich

by James Schroder

Jim Eisenreich was a normal kid until he was six years old. That's when he started to do things like blink his eyes without stopping and clear his throat over and over again. Even though the other kids made fun of him, they all wanted him on their team when it was time to play baseball because he was the best player around. He played baseball all through school and when he went to college in Minnesota, where he was from. Everyone knew there was something different about him, but nobody, not even Jim or his parents, knew what it was.

After college, Jim was drafted by the Minnesota Twins in 1980, spent two years in the minor leagues, and joined the major league club in 1982. That's when things got pretty bad. As he stood in the outfield at Fenway Park in Boston during a game with the Red Sox, his body began jerking wildly. The crowd saw what was happening and started to call him names and yell, "Shake! Shake! Shake!" at him. Jim couldn't continue. He walked off the field and was put on the disabled list, even though no one knew what was wrong. Jim tried again the next year, but only played two games before going on the disabled list. The next year he played twelve games and then basically gave up. Playing baseball was the one thing he loved to do most in the world, but he just couldn't play anymore.

Jim vowed to find out what was wrong with him. He went to doctor after doctor and most of them told him his problem was in his head. What they meant was that he was crazy. Jim Eisenreich wasn't crazy, but the problem did turn out to be in his head—in his brain, to be precise. Three years after he played his last game as a Minnesota Twin, a doctor diagnosed Jim with Tourette's syndrome, a disorder that, according to my research, originates in the brain and causes people sometimes to move their bodies uncontrollably or to say things over and over. (And sometimes to repeat swear words.)

Tourette's isn't really one particular disease; it's a collection of behaviors that can occur on their own or at the same time someone has other problems (like attention deficit disorder). It usually starts before someone is eighteen, tends to happen to boys more than girls, and sometimes goes away on its own by the time a person is twenty-five. Having Tourette's does not mean a person is stupid or retarded. A lot of successful people have had Tourette's. Some people even think Mozart had Tourette's. Unlike when Mozart was alive, Tourette's is now controlled by medication.

This is what happened to Jim Eisenreich. His doctor gave Jim medicine to control his tics. Jim started to get better and to play baseball again.

In 1986 the Kansas City Royals bought out Jim's contract for one dollar.[6] Three years later he hit .229, stole twenty-seven bases, and was named the team's Player of the Year. Jim joined the Phillies as a free agent in 1993 and that season got to play in his first World Series. He also played in the 1997 World Series for the Florida Marlins.

Jim was traded to the Los Angeles Dodgers during 1998 and retired from baseball after that season. He had played for five teams during fifteen seasons. He now travels around the country talking about Tourette's, and runs the Jim Eisenreich Foundation for Children with Tourette Syndrome.[7]

---

6. See www.tourettes.org/about_jim.html.
7. Jim Eisenreich Foundation for Children with Tourette Syndrome, P.O. Box 953, Blue Springs, MO 64013.